HER BEST SHOT

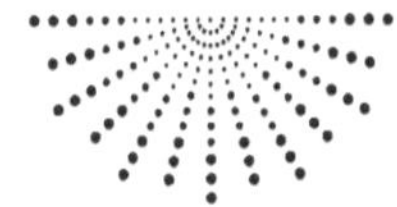

SHANNYN SCHROEDER

This novella was originally published in 2014. I had done research for the characters in the book. However, I used a racial slur. At the time, I did not (even with my research) realize that it was considered a slur. I knew it wasn't complementary, but I didn't do a good enough job. For this I am sorry. I apologize to anyone who read the earlier version and was hurt by my words. All uses and references have been edited out of this version.

CONTENTS

ISBN-13: 978-1-950640-06-5

CHAPTER ONE

Layla Sharpe left the office complex and held her composure until she reached her car. She looked discreetly over her shoulder and then kicked off her heels and danced in the parking lot. Her pencil skirt rode high on her thighs, and after receiving a few stares, she grabbed her phone. Who to call first? Her parents or her best friends?

Her parents would still be at work, so she called Charlie and Felicity on a three-way call. When she had them both on the line and was seated in her car to avoid any more gawking, she blurted, "I had my interview for the summer internship today, and you're *not* going to believe this."

She paused for a deep breath. She wanted to remember the first time she spoke these words.

"And?" Felicity's voiced wobbled across the line.

"And what?" Charlie said. "We know you got the internship. They love you."

Layla's chest swelled with pride. "They offered me a job instead of the internship."

Her words were met with a high-pitched squeal from Felicity and a "holy shit" from Charlie.

"I can't wait to tell you guys all about it. You're both still going to be home for spring break, right?"

Charlie answered, "I never left, remember?"

Felicity added, "Well, that was the plan, but don't you think in light of your excellent news, we should celebrate? We should all meet up for a proper spring break. Let's go somewhere touristy and get drunk and have fun."

Layla straightened in her seat. Was that really Felicity talking? Partying she would expect from Charlie, but never Felicity.

"Okay, who are you? Hey, Layla, are you sure you dialed right?" Charlie asked.

"Yes, she dialed right, smart-ass. Every year we talk about going somewhere and doing something fun. This is our last spring break. After this, we're all out in the real world. We might be scattered all over the country for our jobs. I heard a girl talking about going to South Padre Island in Texas. Let's go."

Layla considered her options. She'd always wanted to drive cross-country on a road trip. This might be her only chance for a long time. "I'm in. I'm going to drive starting right now."

"Great. I'll change my flight. Good-bye, Chicago; hello, Texas. What about you, Charlie?"

"I have a con planned for next weekend."

Layla rolled her eyes. Charlie and her damn comic book/superhero/video game conventions. "So come for the first part of the week."

Charlie became suspiciously quiet.

"Charlotte, we hear you breathing. What's going on?" Layla asked.

"I don't want to take away from your exciting news."

"Spit it out."

"I think Ethan has something special planned for this week."

Ethan. What a jerk. Layla had no idea what Charlie saw in him. He believed her love of computers and games was a strange hobby that she'd outgrow. He had no idea.

"It won't be the same without you." It might do Charlie some good to get out of the house, away from games and from Ethan.

"I know, but you guys go ahead and have fun. I expect you to have my share of fun too. Especially Felicity. Get that girl laid."

"Hey, *that girl* is listening. What makes you think I need to get laid?"

Charlie snickered. "When was the last time you had an orgasm with someone other than yourself?"

"Some of us have discriminating taste."

"Yeah, and some of us are too shy to speak to anyone with a dick."

"Now, girls . . . " Layla interrupted.

"Whatever, Charlie. Look, I'm going to book us a room. I don't know how easy it's going to be since it's last minute, but I'll find something and text you the info."

Layla thought briefly of her bank account. "Make it a cheap room."

"I've got you covered. Consider it a graduation present."

Felicity was the only one of the three of them who had grown up with money. They'd all met at the same prep school. While Layla and Charlie had been there on scholarship, Felicity's parents had paid full boat. Felicity was used to being generous with her money. Sometimes too generous.

"I can pay."

"I know you can. Let me treat you. In return, you can teach me to pick up men."

Layla felt her smile broaden. "Deal."

They said their good-byes, and Layla started her car. She'd only packed a backpack before leaving school. She'd spent the night in Maryland to be ready for the interview, but now she wasn't sure what to do. Should she just hit the road and buy a few essentials on the way, or should she return to school in Boston and pack properly?

All the nervous energy answered for her. She'd change into something more comfortable and hit the road. She had enough packed for a couple of days. She always overplanned that way.

Screw it. It was time for fun and spontaneity. Everything she'd been working toward was within her grasp. Graduating at the top of her class, a sweet job offer working in the field she wanted most, and now a surprise vacation. What more could she ask for?

If she hurried, she could miss rush-hour traffic and log some miles before stopping for dinner. She'd spend the night wherever she landed.

Her mother would kill her if she knew. She hated Layla's being so far away for school. The thought of Layla driving halfway across the country alone would probably give her mother hives. Maybe she'd just confide in Dad and let him break the news to Mom. *That* was a plan.

Layla stopped at the first gas station she found, filled up, and changed into her favorite pair of jeans and T-shirt, one of her many geek-girl shirts. It said, "Welcome to the Dork Side. We Have Pi." Right before she left for college, she had begun collecting math-geek T-shirts. They fit her personality, and they were always a good conversation starter. She couldn't begin to count the number of times a guy had asked her to explain her shirt (sometimes because he didn't understand; other times because he thought she didn't).

Plus, the shirts gave her an identity. She didn't have to worry about people trying to figure out which friend she was—the smart one, the pretty one, the friendly one; her shirt said it all. Layla grabbed a ginormous Coke and a Snickers bar and tried to figure out the best route to Texas. She sat in her car and played with the GPS on her phone. She wanted to take a scenic route, but not one that would put her in the middle of nowhere. She was a city girl, after all.

With her GPS programmed, she headed south. Miles flew by, and her mind enjoyed the peace. At least for a while. She planned how to tell her parents about the job offer. Although she hadn't accepted it yet, she would. As a sophomore, she had set her sights on working as a cryptographer for the NSA. It was the stuff of spy novels without the danger.

When she stopped for dinner, she called her parents, who offered cautious congratulations. She heard her mother's fretting at the thought of Layla's working so far away. Layla opted not to exacerbate her mother's nervousness and only told them that she wouldn't be home for spring break. She allowed them to infer that she was staying on campus. She told herself that the omission would be good practice for keeping government secrets.

After checking into a cheap motel for the night, Layla received a text from Felicity with the resort information. With thoughts of the beach and sexy guys, Layla slept for a few hours, but was woken by dreams of working in an office, shuffling papers, and staring at a computer screen in a cubicle, boring herself to tears. The office had no windows, just rows of partitions, where she could hear, but not see other people clicking on keyboards and answering phones.

She took a quick shower to clear her head and decided to hit the road early. Once in her car, thoughts of the gray, dreary dream haunted her. There was no way her new job would be that boring, right? She would be faced with numbers and problems to solve every day. She drove and tried to think of sunnier subjects.

The tightness in her chest was a telltale sign of an impending anxiety attack. She hadn't had one since just before high school graduation, but she'd never forget the feeling. A tingling itchiness invaded her limbs.

Pulling over to the shoulder of the highway, Layla rolled down her windows to get some semi-fresh air. She closed her eyes and breathed deeply. Freaking out over graduating and starting a new job made no sense. This was part of life. Everyone did it. She shook her head, turned up the radio, and pulled back into traffic.

Growing up was a little scary. But she had this week when she didn't have to think about it. For spring break, she could be a girl without a plan, one who didn't know anxiety.

So much for not knowing anxiety. Layla walked down the busy street in Atlanta looking for the nearest bar. She needed a drink.

After a leisurely drive through the mountains and taking time to enjoy the beauty of rural North Carolina, Layla had been feeling better. Then she had pulled into Atlanta and everything went to hell. Her car just stopped. She probably shouldn't have ignored the clunking while she was in the mountains. She sat at the side of the road waiting for a tow truck for a couple of hours. Not that she didn't have offers, from a variety of good old boys, to take her wherever she wanted to go.

Because it was Saturday afternoon, the mechanic had told her straight-out that nothing would be done on her car until Monday, but he'd promised to call her with a diagnosis before the end of the day. She had barely stopped herself from telling him to just fix it no matter what. Although she didn't like being stranded in Georgia, she wasn't going to pay an exorbitant amount of money out of desperation for her hand-me-down car.

Pulling her backpack higher on her shoulder, she stood still for a moment and allowed her eyes to adjust to the dim interior of the first bar she found. It was a dive, but there was a decent-sized crowd. Unfortunately, it wasn't her kind of crowd. They were mostly men and mostly grubby-looking. Even the younger ones had a roughness about them.

Layla figured it was par for the course. All she wanted to do was drown her sorrows in some beer and then pass out until her car was fixed. Maybe she could salvage part of her break. She shot a text to Felicity to let her know about the car.

After ordering a light beer at the bar, Layla walked around to find a spot to drink alone. In the back, she found a few men playing pool at the two tables. She grabbed a chair and sat with her back to the wall so she could watch the players. No one seemed to take notice of her presence.

Within moments, one player easily stood out as the man to beat. He was tall, over six feet, with long dark hair pulled back into a ponytail. He wore a T-shirt that looked intentionally too tight, showing off defined muscles, as if to say, "Don't fuck with me." He didn't chat with the other player. The only sounds he made were to call his shots. He was smooth and efficient, and fun to watch as he cleared the table.

Especially when he bent over in front of her. Maybe being stuck in Atlanta for the night wouldn't be so bad if all the guys were this nice to look at. With the eight ball sunk, the man stood and collected the money sitting on the edge of the table. The loser walked away, and another guy took his place, putting his twenty on the edge.

This second player was better than the first, but Mr. Nice Ass stayed ahead. After a while, Layla began to wonder if he was just toying with his competition, like a cat playing with its prey. He let the other man sink a few balls and then returned to clear the table. Again, he sank the eight ball and swiped the cash.

The man was a pool hustler.

After the second loser left, the man looked around, his gaze landing on her. His eyes, a gray-green, weren't pretty, but were mesmerizing. Something about the contrast against his olive skin.

He pointed his pool cue at her. "Are you going to sit there staring all night, or are you going to play?"

"Me? I'm not stupid enough to play pool with a hustler. My day's been crappy enough. I don't need to lose anything else."

He stalked closer to her. "I'm not a hustler. Hustlers pretend to be bad and then show their true ability to win big. Make no mistake. I'm always good."

As he spoke, she listened to the cadence of his voice. He didn't have the accent that the other men had. She couldn't tell where he was from.

"Thanks for the vocabulary lesson. I still have better things to do with twenty bucks than lose it to you, especially since I've only played pool a handful of times."

He took another step closer. Close enough that she could touch him if she wanted, but he kept enough distance so she wasn't crowded. "How about you buy me a beer, and I'll give you a lesson?"

She had nothing else going on, and a game of pool with a sexy stranger might be fun. "You're on. What'll you have?"

He tilted his head toward her bottle. "Whatever you're having is fine."

She grabbed her backpack and went back to the bar to buy a couple more beers. When she returned, he had the balls racked and ready to go. She placed her backpack on her chair and grabbed a cue stick. Layla handed him a bottle and said, "I'm Layla."

He took the bottle from her, allowing his thumb to brush over her fingers. "Thanks, Layla. I'm Phin."

The simple touch sent a jolt of pleasure up her arm and down her center. He took a swig of beer, and she watched his throat work as he swallowed. She licked her lips, and when he reached past her to put his bottle on the table, her mouth went dry. This man was like a walking orgasm. He didn't have to say anything, and she wanted to go for a test run.

"Let's get started." He moved back to the pool table. "Do you want to break, or should I?"

"Go ahead." She stood to the side, gripping her cue stick.

He leaned forward, and the roped muscles of his forearms flexed as he made his shot. He sank a solid-colored ball, but because she was too busy watching him and not the table, she didn't see which one.

"Do you know the rules?"

She nodded. "You sank a solid, so I have stripes. Call what pocket I'm aiming for and get the balls in. Don't sink the eight until the end."

"First rule, watch the table." He followed this with a warm grin that told her he liked to tease.

Two could play at that. He leaned over for his next shot, and she shifted closer to him and leaned on the edge. The muscle in his jaw twitched and he straightened.

He carefully set down his stick and walked behind her. Before she could register what was happening, Phin had picked her up by her hips and a squeal popped from her throat. He set her down a couple of feet back.

When she had her balance, she crossed her arms and looked up at him. "What are you doing?"

He cleared his throat before answering. "You can't lean on the table during another player's shot."

She gave him a wide-eyed look. "How else am

I supposed to learn? I paid for a lesson, and if you think that watching you win is going to teach me, you're wrong. I might not look like much, but I'm pretty competitive. You'll beat me, but I'm a quick study."

"I'll keep that in mind. Now stay back." He pointed his stick in her direction. "Seven, side pocket." He tapped the pocket he aimed for as if she couldn't figure it out. The ball thunked in and he continued. "Three, corner pocket."

This time, as he leaned over, Layla strolled to the other side of the table. He didn't move his head, but she felt him staring at her. He struck the cue ball, but it angled and glanced off the three, missing his intended target. "Your shot."

Layla stared at the table, trying to decide what would be her easiest shot, instead of taking another peek at his ass. She walked around the corner to get a full picture of where the balls sat and where they should go. When she returned to Phin's side, she asked, "Fifteen in the corner. That's my best bet, right?"

$\mathcal{P}$hin nodded. He didn't know what he'd been thinking, offering to play with this girl. She had trouble written all over her. He'd noticed her as soon as she had entered the room. First, this bar rarely had pretty girls walk through; second, she paid as much attention to the game as she did to the players, so he wasn't quite sure what she was looking for. Her short, dark hair was a mess, and she wasn't wearing any makeup. She wore her clothes comfortably, and he liked the *Star Wars* joke on her shirt.

The problem was he'd managed to avoid trouble for a long time.

She was different, and that alone caught his attention. Most women would feign interest in the game to hit on him. Not Layla. She walked around the table and attempted to set up her shot. Leaning forward, she awkwardly tried to balance the stick in her hands.

This was the part he loved most about helping a girl learn to play pool. He stood behind her and circled his arms around her body. With his left hand, he formed hers into a steady bridge and set the cue on it. Then he grasped her hips to straighten them. He forced his fingers not to linger.

A subtle shift of her shoulders let him know that she wasn't impervious to his touch. He leaned close to her ear while using his right hand to lower the back end of the cue. "Keep the cue parallel to the table. Go in on an angle and the ball will skip and hop. Use a strong, steady stroke. Follow through once you commit."

Her breath hitched a little on the way in, and Phin wondered if she would sound like that in bed. He didn't move, but waited for her to take her shot.

Layla twisted a half turn and smiled up at him. Her lips were within reach if he lowered his head. "You're leaning on the table during my turn. Stay back."

Then she hip-checked him. She wasn't nearly big enough nor strong enough to really move him, but considering his mind was on tasting her lips, she caught him off guard and he tilted.

He took the hint and stepped back. Maybe he was off his game and she really wasn't interested in anything other than a game of pool.

Phin crossed his arms and waited. Layla proceeded to wiggle her hips and reposition herself the way he'd shown her. She easily sank the ball and sent him a cocky grin.

"One ball doesn't make you a winner."

"I know, but it's more than you thought I was

capable of." She eyed the table. "Twelve off the side and into opposite side pocket."

"You sure?" The shot wasn't impossible, but unlikely for a beginner.

"I think so. Go hard or go home, right?"

"That's one option."

She winked. "It's the only option."

Phin expected her to swing into the shot and miss. Instead she moved around the table studying the placement of all the balls. She lowered herself and shifted on her feet. He could almost see the figures she was trying to create. He'd seen it before—people who approached the game with a method, like an equation.

That's not how Phin played. He did what felt right. Although his moves made sense, his gut led his decisions. Layla straightened and walked the table again. He started to lose his patience, the one skill he needed to hone. In tournament play, plenty of players moved slowly, taking in every option before making a move. Phin preferred to play pool like a game of speed chess. Snap judgments based on his opponent and the field of play. His mind always jumped a few steps ahead, seeing where balls would roll before being struck.

Most players couldn't imagine what would happen and where the balls would land, so they plotted and planned their shots. Layla was a plotter. She examined each angle, and he enjoyed watching her.

Layla lined up her shot, and he knew she had it before the stick made contact with the cue ball. He didn't need to look as he heard the chink of ball meeting ball, followed by the padded thud of the ball hitting the side before the final clunk of it falling into the pocket. Instead, he watched Layla's face, especially her midnight blue eyes. She followed the twelve off the side, but then lifted her gaze to meet his. She knew she had it.

Arrogance would never win the game. She lifted one eyebrow as if to say, "Told you." This time, she only walked around the table once, getting a little too close when she passed him, before calling her shot. "Nine, corner pocket."

Again, he watched her set up the shot, and, before the cue ball made contact, he knew she'd blown it. Her eyes narrowed at the nine that bounced in the opposite direction. At least she didn't scratch.

She held her cue in front of her chest, the line bisecting her, making it difficult to do anything other than focus on her breasts. He reread her shirt and began to think about pie. And Layla naked.

"So what'd I do wrong?"

"Huh?"

She moved the stick in order to walk, breaking his concentration on her chest. She neared him and asked, "Why did I miss?"

"You got cocky and it cost your concentration. The first two worked, and, although the third shot should've been an easy one, you lost your stance and your bridge was sloppy. You didn't have enough control. You can't ever spend time thinking about the last shot. Worst case, you focus on the shot at hand. Best case, you think two or three shots ahead."

She tilted her head and narrowed her eyes. "How am I supposed to plan ahead if I don't know where the balls will land?"

"You predict. Look, if I try to hit the three into the corner, it's going to push others out of the way. Where are they going to roll? That's how I'll set up my next shot. I can force those balls to land where I want based on how I hit them." He took a swig of his beer. Layla didn't respond, but she absorbed what he said. He saw the understanding in her eyes and didn't need the verbal confirmation.

"I want the five to move to the left, so I'm going to hit it on the right side with a little spin. I don't want it to shoot far, just enough." He leaned down and took the shot. The three swooshed into the corner pocket, and the five lined up exactly where he wanted.

Layla's face suddenly brightened. "I got it!" She walked to the opposite corner and rattled off possibilities.

He nodded and then cleared the solids without looking up. Layla didn't crowd him and she'd stopped flirting. When the eight fell into the pocket, he straightened and laid his cue on the table. Layla didn't acknowledge him. Her gaze stayed locked on the remaining balls. Maybe she was so competitive that she was a sore loser.

"Can I clear the table?"

Her question surprised him and his face must've reflected that.

"I know you won, big surprise, but I think I see the shots I'd take and want to try."

"Knock yourself out. I'm going to get another beer. You want one?"

"Sure. Thanks."

Phin went to the bar and grabbed the beers. When he returned, she was racking the balls.

"Another game?" Layla asked.

"Sure. What are we playing for?"

"I'm a poor college student. I'm still not going to pay you twenty dollars."

"Not confident in your ability, huh?"

"I'm confident in my ability, but you're a shark. My money's staying in my pocket."

Phin moved closer and handed her a beer. "So what do you have in mind?"

She tilted her head, as appeared to be habit, and said, "A kiss. I've never kissed a guy with hair longer than mine."

He reached out and ran his hand over the back of her head, where there wasn't enough hair to grab. "Not hard to do. Besides, if you want a kiss, all you have to do is ask."

"Uh-uh. It's a fair wager."

"What do I get if I win?" Although he'd be fine paying up as the loser, Layla was looking relaxed enough that he might be able to get more than a kiss.

"What do you want?" She took a drink and added, "Before you answer, there's no way in hell I'm playing strip pool."

Hmmm . . . He hadn't given that a thought, but eight balls, eight articles of clothing . . . could be fun. The jeans would be the first to go—he wanted to know if she was a thong or a bikini girl.

Suddenly her hand was in his face. "Yoo-hoo. Get your mind out of the gutter."

"The gutter's a fun place." He shook his head and cleared the image of Layla in skimpy underwear. "If I win, you buy the next round."

"Deal." She extended her hand.

He took it, enjoying the soft, smooth skin, so pale against his hand, and leaned forward. "You make me want to lose."

Her lips twitched. "You break. I don't know how to do that right."

He set his bottle on the edge and walked away.

"So, where are you from?"

Leaning toward the cue ball, he asked, "What do you mean?"

"Where are you from? You don't sound like you're from Georgia, but I can't quite place your accent."

"I don't have an accent. I'm from nowhere. I move around a lot."

"But where's home?"

The cue ball cracked into the triangle. The four flew to the corner and disappeared. Solids again. "I don't have a home."

"Everyone has a home. Where's your family?"

He shrugged. "Probably still in New York. They move a lot too."

"I'm from Chicago, but I go to school at MIT."

MIT—a brainy chick. "Seven, side." Before he

lined up the shot, he asked, "So what are you doing in Georgia?"

"It's spring break. I'm supposed to be celebrating with my friend on South Padre Island in Texas. Unfortunately, I only made it this far and my car broke down. I'm waiting to hear from the mechanic to see what's wrong and how long it'll take to fix it."

He looked up at her. "Who's the mechanic?"

She wrinkled her face like it was a crazy question. "Some guy named Steve down the street."

Phin relaxed a little. He knew many mechanics would take one look at her bright face and see a mark. "When's Steve supposed to call?"

She shrugged. "He said he'd call before he left for the night."

"You're in luck. I happen to work for Steve. I'll find out." He stepped away from the table and pulled out his phone. When Steve answered, Phin said, "Hey, Steve, a car was towed in a little while ago for a girl."

"Yeah, Bill brought the car in. Hot chick. A little clueless about her car, though."

"She's with me shooting some pool. What's the diagnosis?"

"Ah, shit. Are you going to ask for a discount so you can get laid?"

"Would it work?"

Steve sighed heavily. "Her transmission needs to be rebuilt. You want to do it on your time, go ahead. It's an old VW Beetle, and she looks broke. Talk to her and see what she wants to do. See you Monday."

Phin shoved his phone into his pocket. Did he want to rebuild her transmission just to get laid? He never worked that hard for a piece of ass.

"Well? What did he say?" Her eyes were so wide and hopeful, like she really believed it would be a small fix.

"Your transmission's shot and needs to be rebuilt."

"Fuck." The single word wasn't angry, but full of disappointment. "Did he say what it's going to cost?"

Phin shook his head. "Didn't say. Let's play." He picked up his cue and went back to work.

Layla ignored the table and texted instead. The *tick-tick-tick* of her tapping annoyed him and he missed his next shot. He didn't know why his concentration was so off today. He'd played with plenty of women before, most of whom were at least flashing cleavage, yet Layla distracted him every other turn.

"You're up."

She nodded absently. "I'm just letting my friend know that I'm going to be stuck here for a while longer than expected."

An enormous sigh lifted her shoulders, and she put her phone back in her pocket.

"Come on, it's not that bad. Show me your stuff. I want to see you win so you can have your way with me."

This brought a smile to her lips. She rolled her head and shrugged. "You're on."

Her determination returned and she set to sinking balls on the table. She sank three before missing. She hadn't been kidding. She was a quick study.

"I'm beginning to think you're the hustler."

"If I was a hustler, I'd be playing for more than a kiss and a beer."

"We can up the stakes whenever you want."

"Thanks, but I'll play it safe." She drank her beer and watched him drop balls.

Unfortunately, he couldn't get at the eight without trouble, so he'd have to wait a turn to win. Layla stalked the table and planned her shots. She sank another three before missing again. She set her cue down. "I'll go get the beer."

"I haven't won yet. It's unsportsmanlike to concede a game before it's over."

She crossed her arms and one eyebrow shot up.

"And you better stay and make sure I don't cheat." He leaned over and sent the eight home.

"Shocking."

"Don't be a sore loser." He grabbed the waistband of her jeans and drew her closer.

"What are you doing?"

"Giving you a consolation prize."

He slid his hand around the curve of her hip and applied enough pressure to bring her even closer. She wasn't tiny, but she was short enough that he had to lower himself to align all the right parts.

She reached up and clasped her hands behind his head. A quick smile and then she was tugging at the rubberband holding his hair back.

His hair fell forward, but she ran her fingers through it and pulled his face closer.

Their lips touched gently and, for a moment, he thought she'd back off. He held tight and shifted for a better angle. She opened her mouth to welcome him. When his tongue met hers, her fingers tightened in his hair. He deepened the kiss, tasting the beer they'd had and sweetness that was her.

Phin turned Layla and pinned her against the table with his hips. She rocked against him and sucked on his lower lip. His fingers itched to shove her shirt up and explore, but he remembered they were in the bar, so he pulled away.

Her eyes fluttered before opening. "Mmm. If that was what I got as a loser, I can't wait to see what I get when I win. I'll get those beers now."

Phin didn't move. He had no doubt she felt the bulge in his pants, but he didn't necessarily want the rest of the bar to see his hard-on. "What's your hurry?"

"If I keep standing here, this close, we won't stop at a kiss." She pressed a hand to his chest, pushing him back.

He let her walk around him without following. He was doing a few quick math problems in his head to refocus his energy when Layla shrieked behind him. He spun and saw her frantically shoving chairs away from the table.

"Oh my God. Where is it?"

"What?"

"My backpack. I left it right here and it's gone."

"It probably fell." He walked over to the table, but he had a bad feeling. It wasn't like the bar was filled with thugs, but people took any opportunity afforded them.

"Shit. It's gone. Someone stole it." Layla thunked her head against the table.

"Did it have anything important in it?"

"Everything, except my license and my phone. All my clothes, my wallet, my phone charger."

Who the hell traveled with all of their possessions in a backpack and then left it unattended? "Why would you leave it alone if it held everything you own?"

Her head shot up so fast, he thought it might fly off. "What was I supposed to do? Keep it on my back while we played pool? Don't talk to me like I'm stupid. I left it on a chair in plain view so I could keep an eye on it."

Layla spun and pointed a finger at his chest. "This is all your fault."

He laughed. "My fault?"

"If you hadn't distracted me with 'Let's play pool,' and then the flirting and the touching. And let's not forget the sexy kiss to make my brain foggy enough that I couldn't see anything, much less focus on my bag."

"It's my fault you can't keep your hormones in check?" This was getting good. He crossed his arms and waited. Layla was pissed and she looked damn fine like that.

"You're probably in on it. You probably have a partner who grabbed my stuff while you distracted me."

"Whoa." He put his hand up to stop her tirade. It was one thing to accuse him of distracting her because he had sex on his mind, but it was another to accuse him of being a thief. He'd left all of that behind a long time ago. "I do *not* steal."

"And why should I believe you?"

Phin stepped closer and leaned his face within inches of hers. "Because if I wanted to steal from you, I sure as hell wouldn't still be standing here. And you can bet that the cash and phone in your pocket would be gone too."

Her face fell. "That really doesn't make me feel any better." She moved back and sat on the stool. "I have nothing. I hadn't even gotten around to getting a room for tonight. I have to cancel my credit cards, and I barely have enough cash in my pocket to buy dinner. What the hell am I supposed to do for clothes? My favorite shirts were in that bag. And my car . . . Fuck. I'm sure Steve's going to fix that for free, right?"

Layla held her phone in her hand looking utterly confused. Her anger and spunk sputtered out.

Shit. Even he wasn't enough of an asshole to leave her sitting there like that. "Go check the bathroom."

"Huh?"

"I'll check the men's room; you check the women's. Chances are if someone here took your bag, he or she would've grabbed the wallet and dumped the rest. It doesn't sound like you had anything else of value in the bag."

She slid from the stool and moped toward the back. He trailed behind and tried not to study her delicious ass. Before they even got to the bathrooms, Layla darted forward. "My bag!"

Her backpack lay by the rear exit, contents spilling all over the floor. Layla knelt on the floor beside the bag and dumped everything out. She reached deep into each pocket, almost turning them inside out. "No wallet."

Phin snorted. "Did you really believe it would still be there?"

"No. But I kinda hoped." She set to the task of refolding her clothes.

Phin glimpsed something purple and shimmery and bent over to pick it up. The slippery scrap of material slid between his fingers as he handed the panties to Layla. She was a bikini girl.

She snatched the panties from him and shoved them into the bag. He offered a hand to help her off the floor. She eyed his hand suspiciously, but accepted it. After shrugging both backpack straps over her shoulders, she pulled her phone back out. "Thanks for the game. I have to make some calls and figure out what I'm going to do."

Damn she looked pitiful. She wanted a fun spring break and instead she was stranded in a town by herself and she'd just been robbed. "I have a couch."

She froze and looked into his eyes. "Good for you. I have a phone."

"Smart-ass. You can crash on my couch until you get your shit straightened out."

"Why would you offer that? You don't even know me."

Phin offered because he'd been in similar situations over the years. Shit, he was still pretty much alone wherever he went. Layla couldn't manage to have a couple of beers without almost losing everything. He couldn't imagine what would happen to her if he didn't offer. "I have a soft spot for strays."

"Thanks, but it's not a good idea." She hitched the bag higher on her shoulders, but didn't move.

"You're not going to get a better offer. Lots of shitbags out there."

"How do I know you're not one?"

"You don't. But what are your other options? Sleep on a park bench?"

$\mathcal{L}$ayla thought about her options. She could call her parents, but then she'd have to admit to lying to them in the first place. Mom would have a coronary and probably be on the first plane. Felicity would send her cash and book a room for her. Layla checked her watch. Felicity was on a plane headed to Texas. She wouldn't land for a couple of hours. Maybe Layla could just hang out with Phin for a while until she could get hold of Felicity.

"Come on. I won't bite. Unless you're into that sort of thing."

Layla just stared at him, unwilling to admit to the thrill his comment sent through her.

"It was a joke. I didn't offer you my bed. My couch is safe. I'll even sleep with clothes on if it'll make you feel better."

She immediately imagined him strolling around naked. Not a bad way to spend her evening. "Gimme your driver's license."

"Why?"

"Because I'm going to take a picture of it and send it to everyone I know, so that if I go missing, they'll know who to hunt down." She extended her hand. If he wouldn't let her see his license, the decision would be made.

He pulled out a battered black leather wallet and slid the license from its sleeve. She took it and snapped a picture. Then she took one of Phin. Phineas Marks. She'd assumed Finn had been his whole name. Finn looked cool. Phineas sounded kind of geeky. Who would've thought the geek girl would have the cool name and the hottie would have the geek name? "Phineas, huh?"

"It's from a TV show my mom watched when she was a kid. Can I have my license back?"

She handed him the card and sent a text to Felicity and Charlie. As unwise as it might've seemed, Layla convinced herself going with Phin was okay. She'd had one-night stands with stranger men than him and worried less.

A moment later her phone bleeped with a text message from Charlie: **Mmmm…cute! Have fun.**

"Do you want to have another beer or do you want to get out of here?"

"Whatever you want. I'm following you." Layla inhaled deeply to keep the anxiety at bay. The weight was returning to her chest, and she *really* didn't want to have a freakout meltdown here. Definitely not in front of a sexy guy like Phin.

"I'm ready to go. We'll grab some dinner on the way. Burgers good?"

Layla nodded. Phin led the way out of the bar and to a pickup truck. It was beat up with some dings and scratches, but clean. She hopped in, putting her backpack between her and Phin. He didn't say anything as he started the engine and pulled out.

She didn't know what to think of him. He hadn't spoken much at all, yet he'd offered a place to stay. It didn't quite match his tough-guy attitude with the muscles and tight T-shirt. While he drove, she studied him from the corner of her eye. He'd retied his hair, but a few strands escaped the band and swept across his cheekbone. His square jaw was smooth, but she saw the hint of stubble.

Beautiful. That was the perfect word to describe him.

"You already took a picture. Why not look at that?" His eyes hadn't left the road. But when a smirk formed, he glanced at her.

"You're pretty nice to look at. 3D is always better than a picture."

He pulled into a drive-thru and they ordered burgers and fries. When Layla handed him some cash, he pushed it away. "Keep your money."

"You're already giving me a place to stay. I can pay for my dinner."

"Don't worry about it."

He drove on and Layla picked fries out of the bag. She'd always been a stress eater, and if any day qualified, this one certainly did.

When he turned the corner, they were driving back past the bar and toward the mechanic's shop. As if knowing she would question it, he said, "I live in an apartment behind the shop. It's cheap and gives Steve extra money. And since I didn't have to sign a lease, it makes things easy when I'm ready to move on."

"How often do you move on?"

"I usually stay in one place through the winter. I like the south for that. The rest of the year... I don't know. I move every couple of months. New town, new faces, new opportunities."

"So you're a mechanic by day and pool shark by night wherever you go?"

"Sometimes. During the summer, I try to get outdoor work. Roofs, windows, construction stuff." He parked behind the main shop and opened his door. "I'm up there."

She followed his finger to a space above a regular two-car garage. Not a very big apartment.

Grabbing her backpack and the bag of food, she got out and followed him up the rickety wooden steps. Along the side of the building, it looked like a junkyard: Hunks of metal and wire and barrels lay haphazardly. She hoped the inside wouldn't resemble the outside.

Phin shoved the door open and Layla was pleasantly surprised. They walked into a living room-kitchen combo that was clean, and from there she saw two other doors, one each, she assumed, for the bedroom and bathroom. The space was pretty bare. A futon sat against one wall facing a flat-screen TV mounted on the wall. A small cube acted as a table in between the two. A pole lamp stood in the corner beside the futon. That was it. Nothing on the walls or the floor.

Nothing personal. Nothing to show that this was Phin's place.

Layla set her phone on the kitchen counter and the bag of food on the makeshift table. She placed her backpack next to the futon. She and Phin settled next to each other on the futon. The silence grated on her. "So why do you move around so much?"

"Just do."

"What about your family? You said they move around too."

"They do."

Not much of a talker. "And? Why do they move? Military? Jobs?"

He swallowed a huge bite of burger. "I guess you could say it's work."

She sank her teeth into the juicy burger and thought about that. "Why aren't you with your family anymore?"

He just stared at her.

"Too personal? I'm just curious. If you want to keep your shroud of mystery intact, by all means."

That earned her a smile. "I had a weird up-bringing. I got tired of that life."

"You just said that you still move around every couple of months. How is that different?"

She picked at her fries, more fascinated by Phin than hungry.

"I guess it's not really. Not yet. My family had certain expectations that I wasn't willing to live with. So I left."

"Don't you keep in touch?"

He shook his head and stood, crumpling up

his trash. "When you leave, you're gone for good. No longer part of the family."

Layla watched him walk across the small room, and her heart broke a little bit. As much as her parents made her crazy with their dreams and expectations for her, she couldn't imagine ever walking away and never contacting them again. She set her food on the table, her appetite gone.

"Shit. You look like someone just kicked your puppy. It's not a big deal. It was my choice to leave. I wanted a different life and I'm going to get it. I travel from tournament to tournament, playing pool. It's a good way to make money. The next big one is in Vegas in a couple of months." He eyed the burger left on the paper. "Are you done with that?"

She nodded and watched, amazed, as he picked it up and polished it off. "So you're going to leave Atlanta and go to Vegas."

"Yeah."

"Sounds like a fun life. Traveling all over, no demands, no expectations. Pick up and go whenever you want. I've always wanted to travel across the country. It sounds great." She wondered what her life would be like if she just walked away from everything. If she said no to a demanding job with the NSA, hell, if she didn't even finish school. She shook her head at the crazy thought. The stress was definitely catching up to her.

"My life has its moments. Like rescuing a beautiful, stranded girl in a bar. I count that as a good moment." He settled on the couch with her and stretched an arm along the back behind her head. "So what's your major?"

"Math and computer science."

He had a strange smile on his face that she couldn't decipher. "What?" she asked.

"It's a pickup line I never thought I'd use, but it didn't even break your stride. I must be losing my touch."

That was supposed to be a pickup line? "I think you've already picked me up."

He inched closer, his gaze raking down her body. Memories of their kiss washed over her, and her nerves started to tingle. His hand cupped her jaw and brought her face closer. "Is this okay?"

"Yeah."

Phin leaned in and kissed her again. A new kind of tension coiled in her with every sweep of his tongue. His hand left her face and slid down her neck and across her shoulder. Down her arm to where her hand lay in her lap. His fingers caressed her palm with a feather touch before moving on to a firmer grasp of her thigh. The jolt of pleasure caused a hitch in her breath.

He pulled away. "You want to stop?"

Did she? Everything below her waist screamed hell no, but above the neck, she still wasn't so sure. If Felicity didn't call back, she'd be spending the night with this guy. Could she live with that? She focused on his gorgeous face and decided it wouldn't be a hardship. "No."

"No, don't stop, or yes, stop?" His fingers still traced patterns on her thigh, making her hot and wanting. His thumb ran along the inseam of her jeans and her hips wiggled, seeking more.

"No, don't stop."

One side of his mouth lifted. "I was hoping you'd say that."

He moved in again, this time licking and kissing her neck as his hand stroked its way up her thigh. So close. Her panties were wet and she began to move against his hand to ease the tension and desire. He nipped her earlobe and she freed his hair. It fell forward, tickling her hand and her cheek.

His hot breath soaked through her T-shirt and she wanted to feel him on her skin. She pushed against his shoulder to get him to move. She followed as he leaned back against the couch and she straddled him. Once in position, she whipped off her shirt and then leaned over to reclaim his mouth.

Layla loved that the closeness allowed her to grind against his erection. The friction of their jeans added to the delicious warmth that had already taken over the lower half of her body. Excitement licked up from where their bodies joined, and jolts of pleasure shot through her when Phin unclasped her bra and claimed a nipple with his mouth. Her fingers threaded in his hair and held tight. She thrust her torso and hips forward, relishing the feel of his mouth on her breasts, the throbbing at their pelvises.

"Fuck, you're hot." His whisper caressed across her skin, sounding more like a curse than a compliment.

She tugged at his tight shirt, wanting to see the sculpted muscles beneath, and she wasn't disappointed. Where she had admired the strength in his arms while watching him play pool, she could now drool over his chest and abs. So unlike the guys she usually picked up on campus. While she might enjoy their brains, she was all about Phin's body. She dragged her short nails over his stomach and he twitched.

Suddenly he bolted up from the couch with his hands on her ass. She dug her fingers into his shoulders. "What are you doing?"

"Taking you to bed." He strode toward the bedroom with her wrapped around his waist. A moment later, he tossed her on the mattress.

Before she had time to recover from the sudden movement, his hands were at her waistband, unbuttoning and tugging off her jeans. She shimmied as he pulled, but they'd both forgotten about her shoes. He huffed a breath out as if too bothered by the delay. While he yanked at her shoes, she slid her panties down.

When Phin saw her lying naked, he shucked his remaining clothes faster than she could blink. One hand stroked her while the other tweaked a nipple and his mouth sucked the other. She was close to coming. Her hips rocked faster against his hand and she felt his lips curve into a smile.

"Going somewhere without me?"

"Can't wait." Her eyes drifted closed and he slid two fingers into her, causing her to buck harder. While she rode his hand, she heard the unmistakable crinkle of a condom wrapper.

Phin removed his hand and before she could miss the rhythm, he replaced it with his cock, hard and hot. He covered her body with his and stretched her from the inside. He settled against her, and she tried to rock and regain her rhythm to come, but his body prevented her from moving.

He eased out and back again, not allowing her to move. She wrapped her legs around him and tried to pick up the pace, but he wouldn't have it.

The tension coiled deep in her belly and her nerves were taut. She grasped Phin's hair and pulled him to her mouth again. Her tongue stroked his and he moaned. His arms surrounded her and his muscles bulged as he plunged deeper into her. He ground against her and something snapped in her. Her orgasm took her by surprise, and she clutched his head as he lowered his face to her collarbone.

Phin's teeth sank into her skin as she spasmed with release. She felt his arms tremble as he came right after she did. His body, which had been only a breath above hers, now lay heavily on her, but not enough to crush her. Her legs slid away from him, weak and worthless, but her fingers still played with his soft hair while they both attempted to recover.

PHIN LIFTED HIMSELF WITH A GRUNT AND WENT TO the bathroom to dispose of the condom. He glanced over his shoulder at Layla in his bed, soft and sated and still really fucking hot. Totally trouble. And in that moment, he knew he was going to be rebuilding her transmission in order to get in her pants again. He cleaned up and found that he was hungry for more than another round with Layla.

When he emerged from the bathroom, he saw that she hadn't moved and thought she might've fallen asleep.

Her left eye opened and she said, "Are you going to stand there all night staring, or are you going to play?"

Hearing his own words echoed back at him made him laugh. "I'm going to get something to eat. You hungry?"

She pushed herself up to a sitting position. "We just ate."

"I think I burned through that. Maybe next time you should do all the work."

She grabbed a pillow and threw it at him. He caught it easily.

"That was your choice. If you recall, I was on top and poised to do the work on the couch. You changed the venue and position." She stood. "Do you mind if I take a shower? It's been a long day."

"Go ahead." He reached into the closet and tossed her a fresh towel. In the kitchen he pulled out leftover pizza and ate it cold. The water started running, and thought of Layla dripping wet made his dick twitch. He considered how long he'd need to rebuild her transmission. While he contemplated whether he wanted to get deeper into Layla's problems, her phone buzzed. It was text from someone named Felicity.

Plane delayed. Call me and I'll wire money ASAP and get you a hotel room. Be safe.

So Layla wasn't as stranded as he'd thought. She had family or friends or someone who'd rush to help. He missed that feeling. It had been five years since he'd left his family, and that was the one thing he missed the most: knowing that someone always had his back. He might have grown tired of the cons and the scams and the stupid rules that guided his father's decisions, but even now, Phin missed having someone to turn to that he could count on. He kept hoping that feeling would disappear.

Layla stayed in the shower a long time. He'd pulled on some underwear and already drunk one beer waiting for her. He was about to pop the cap off a second when she finally came out with nothing but a towel wrapped around her. Drops of water dripped from the short ends of her hair and skated over her shoulders.

"Sorry. I left my bag in here with my clothes."

He watched as she attempted to hold the towel closed with one hand and dig through her bag with the other. The towel and the bag took turns slipping from her grasp. He twisted the cap off his beer and said nothing, just waited for the frustration to get to her. Finally she said, "Fuck it," and dropped the towel.

Her hand came from her bag clutching a T-shirt and the purple panties he'd picked up from the floor at the bar. Standing in front of him, she stepped into the panties and pulled the shirt over her head, oblivious to how hot she was making him.

Or maybe not. With the Math Ninja shirt in place, she smirked at him and snatched his beer. She took a drink and sat next to him on the couch.

"A text came in while you were in the shower. Someone named Felicity."

Layla hopped up. "Good. She'll get me cash so I can get out of your hair."

He liked the feel of her hands tangled in his hair and was about to tell her so, but she was already dialing.

"She's not answering. I must've missed her. She's probably on the plane now." Layla tapped her toes while clutching her phone. "Hey, Felicity. I'm fine. I'm with a ... friend for now. I was hoping to catch you. I hate to ask for help, but I'm really stuck. I'm not sure when I'm going to be able to get back on the road. Give me a call. Thanks. Love you."

"You can stay here, no strings. I meant it. The futon's yours."

"I appreciate the offer, strange as it is, but I'm not your problem. I can't believe you offered in the first place. Do you have a habit of picking up strays?"

"We were having fun at the bar and it looked like you could use some help. You should call your credit cards in before someone jacks them up."

"I know. I'm on it now." She took her phone into the bedroom and started dialing.

Phin turned on the TV. Nothing grabbed his interest, so he relaxed and let the tones of Layla's quiet voice coast over him from the other room. He felt bad that she was going to miss most of her spring break, but he liked the thought of spending a few days with her.

One thing Layla hadn't thought about when she envisioned his fun life was the loneliness that accompanied him. He couldn't wait for the tournament in Vegas. The purse on that one would give him enough money to live off of for a while. He'd look for the right place to start his new life. One where he'd have roots, friends, neighbors, a place to call home. Maybe he'd even find a nice girl to settle down with and have a family. Then he'd fill that void that had been swallowing him for the past five years.

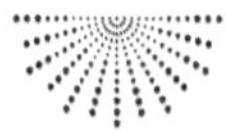

CHAPTER FOUR

Layla hung up after talking to the fourth company and filing a report. Each one offered to ship a new card overnight, for a fee. She chose one and asked Phin for his address. Unfortunately, with it being Saturday night, the earliest she'd get the card would be Tuesday. At least she'd be able to pay for her car when it was ready. What a complete pain in the ass.

She should've waited until after the calls to have sex, because every ounce of relaxation she'd earned had vanished. Back in the living room, Phin remained sprawled on the couch. The hard, lumpy, uncomfortable couch. The beer she'd swiped from him still sat on the table. She took another swig and sat down. He flipped through channels on the TV. Not much of a selection, but he probably wouldn't invest in satellite since he didn't plan to stay in town long.

He tossed the remote in her lap. "You can pick something. I don't watch much TV."

She scrolled through the channels. Nothing grabbed her either. "You got any cards?"

He just looked at her.

"I thought we could play a game or something."

Phin sighed and got off the couch. Then he looked back at her. "Strip poker?"

The man was standing in a pair of boxers and wanted to play strip poker. "That wasn't my plan, but I can do that. The game wouldn't take long since neither of us is wearing much. How about gin rummy instead? I've still got twenty bucks in my pocket."

He stopped rummaging through a drawer in the kitchen. "Hey, babe, when you're looking to scam someone, you let him think the game was his idea. You're too eager, so I know you think you can kick my ass and take my money."

Busted. "I wasn't thinking any such thing," she said, hoping to convey an air of innocence, but he wasn't buying.

"I grew up with con artists. I was scamming people before you were even out of diapers."

"Look at you talking like a grizzled old con artist. You're not much older than I am. I think we were in diapers at the same time. I potty-trained early."

"Overachiever?"

"Is there any other way to be?"

He finally found a deck of cards and returned to her side on the couch. Tossing the cards on the table, he said, "Rummy, huh? I haven't played in a long time. My grandma liked to play."

"It'll come back to you. We can play a couple of hands for practice. I'm not totally heartless." She shuffled the deck. As quickly as he'd beat her at pool, she felt the need to redeem herself.

Layla quickly explained the rules of the game to him, and he nodded.

"Don't we need to write down the score to keep track?"

She pointed to her chest. "Math major, remember? I can keep track in my head."

"No offense, but I prefer to see it in black-and-white. You know, just to be sure."

Her jaw dropped dramatically. "Are you accusing me of being a cheater?"

"You? Never. I'm sure you would never consider doing anything like rubbing up against me or shaking your hips to distract me during my turn."

She smiled. "That was just to keep you on your toes. I was attempting to level the playing field. You're a pool shark and I'm a newbie. I wanted a fair chance."

"Using your feminine wiles is dirty pool."

"Hmm-mmm." She dealt the cards and organized her hand.

Phin found a napkin and wrote two columns, putting their names on the top of each. Layla held her cards high, not sure if she had a tell that would give her away. Phin was far too perceptive and she knew it, which was why she didn't want to play poker with him. She'd lose her pants figuratively and literally.

She schooled her face and focused on the

cards. If she watched closely, she'd beat him. She just had to play her cards right. Now she was thinking in clichés. Giving herself a mental shake, she played her first card.

An hour later, Layla and Phin were slapping cards down faster than either could see. It turned out that Phin's competitive side matched hers. He pushed; she shoved. They trash-talked each other and laughed all the way through. She hadn't had so much fun playing a card game since she had first learned to count cards as a freshman.

Finally, she sent Phin her best seductive smile and splayed her cards on the table. "Gin," she said sweetly.

Judging by the stack of cards he held, he wouldn't be able to catch her.

"You're better than I expected," he said, tossing his cards down without adding them up. "How would you like to collect your winnings?"

He crawled across the couch until he had her pressed against the wooden arm. He stared into her eyes, his lips close to touching hers. She smiled again. "Twenty bucks. I'm broke."

He laughed and put his arms around her, the sound tickling her ear. Phin kissed her neck and ground his hips into hers. The energy between them skyrocketed from playful to sensual in a blink. God, this man was good. She had no problem imagining him as a con artist. His smile and smooth-talking ways drew her to him. And those eyes. They were spooky—laughing one minute and drowning in passion the next—but they never revealed who Phin was.

Her phone rang and Layla moaned. As much fun as she was having, she knew Felicity was calling to rescue her. She shifted to grab the phone, but Phin beat her to it.

Before handing it over, he said, "Stay with me. You have to wait until your car is ready. Stay here."

She took the phone and answered. "Hey, Felicity, hang on a minute." She covered the mouthpiece. Looking at Phin, she asked, "Why?"

"Because we're having fun. Why pay for a hotel when you're just gonna want to sleep with me anyway?"

"You think you're all that."

"Of course, and then some." To prove his point, he slid a hand between her thighs and massaged her muscles, keeping his hand just south of her mound, making her wetter.

She shifted away from his hand and turned her attention to the phone, but his hand was persistent.

"Hi. Thanks for getting back to me so quickly." Was that her talking all breathlessly?

"Hey, Layla, are you okay? What happened?"

Focus on Felicity, not the pleasure waiting in Phin's hand. "My car broke down. The transmission needs to be rebuilt. It's going to take a few days, and then as I was trying to drown my sorrows in a beer, someone stole my wallet. I have twenty bucks to my name." She stopped and looked at Phin. "Make that forty bucks."

He chuckled and lowered his head to her neck. He licked a slow, warm trail up to her ear.

"Tell me what you need," Felicity said. She sounded so far away.

"I have a new credit card being sent. It'll be here Tuesday. In the meantime, I made a friend. His name is Phin. I sent you his picture. Did you get it?"

"Hell, yeah, I did. He's hot. Are you with him now?"

Just then, Phin's hand made it to its destination, and she nearly jumped out of her moist panties. Using his knee, he spread her thighs, which she had been involuntarily clenching, apart. "Yeah, he's here."

"Do you want me to book a hotel for you?"

Layla's brain clouded. Hotel. She was supposed to go to a hotel. But Phin had told her to stay. The rest of her spring break was likely fucked; why not enjoy a few days of his time? Especially when he made her feel this good. "Uh, no, I'm gonna stay here. Phin has a spot for me."

She felt his lips curve in a smile against her collarbone. Asshole. But she couldn't stay mad because her pussy had other ideas. Her breath came faster as he increased the speed of his manipulations, but he had yet to enter her and man, did she want that.

"Are you sure you're okay? You sound funny."

"Yep. Great. Reeeeally great. I'll call you later, okay. Have fun."

"Oh, you're getting busy right now, aren't you?"

Layla giggled.

"Jeez, that's just wrong. Call me later." Felicity

disconnected, and Layla tossed the phone on the floor.

She lifted her hips and yanked her panties off. In the next breath, she pulled her shirt over her head. Somewhere in the back of her mind she knew that lying naked on a stranger's couch should've felt weird, but all she could think was *now.* She needed Phin now.

Phin moved her so she was lying down on the couch and lowered his head to her breasts. As he pulled a nipple roughly into his mouth, he slid two fingers into her. She was so close, but she couldn't form words to tell him what she needed. Layla grabbed Phin's hand and forced his palm against her. With the pressure against her clit and his fingers moving in and out, she exploded. Her thighs clenched tightly on his hand and he bit down on her nipple.

Her hand grasped for something, anything, to hold on to. She grabbed his hair, tunneling her fingers all the way to his scalp, and held tight. Layla rode the waves and spasms until she couldn't move anymore. As she came down from her high, she felt Phin's rigid cock against her thigh. She reached past his boxers and stroked him.

He groaned and laid his head against her chest, not moving. His hand was still against her, his fingers in her, not moving. In her awkward position, she couldn't do much for him. She wanted more, wanted to feel him in her again. She pulled his hair, lifted his face from her chest.

She kissed him hard, thrusting her tongue

into his mouth. Pulling his head back, she pushed his shoulder with her hand until he moved enough that she was on top of him. He'd removed his fingers from her, and she withheld the moan it caused. She straddled him, making his boxers as wet as he'd made her.

Layla continued to kiss him while she rocked and bounced against him, never freeing him from the constraint of the cotton. Teasing him like this made her feel powerful and she enjoyed it. He grabbed her hips and tried to control the rhythm or move her away, she wasn't sure which, but she wasn't giving in.

His fingers dug into the flesh of her ass. "Fuck," he growled.

She leaned close, lifted her hips away from him, and whispered, "How bad do you want it?"

Layla held her hips inches above him but continued their rhythm, determined to make him feel with his hands what his dick was missing. A sheen of sweat coated him and she liked knowing it was because of her. "I think we need a condom." Luckily, she had a couple in her bag. She turned and reached into it.

Turning her back on Phin had been a mistake because she lost the upper hand. He growled again and picked her up. The condom flew from her hand and landed on the couch. Phin pushed her down on her stomach, and she heard the wrapper tear. She struggled to push up, but he wrapped his arm around her waist and entered from behind. The sudden shock of him filling her caused a gasp.

Phin released her waist and, using both hands on her hips, pumped into her wildly. She gripped the arm of the couch to gain some balance, but couldn't hold. He was rough, but careful, and Layla had never been more turned on. Her breath hitched in halting gasps. Phin's right hand slid around and she felt his chest touch her back.

His rhythm slowed. He pinched her nipple and she was able to rise up on her elbows. He bit down on her shoulder and she ground her hips against him, searching for a second orgasm that he was withholding. He had brought her to the edge and then intentionally slowed.

She took a deep breath, forcing air all the way into her lungs, and then said, "Who's being a tease now?"

She bit down on her lip and tried moving her hips, but Phin just laughed. His other arm reached around her and he pulled her up on her knees against him. The fingers that had been pinching her left her breast and moved to her clit. He flicked at it twice and Layla was spiraling again. Stars burst behind her closed eyes and every muscle in her legs ached. She felt like a noodle, but Phin continued his assault.

He rubbed and caressed and bit her, until each nerve was exposed and exploited. Just when she didn't think she could handle more, Phin released her, and she flopped forward on the couch. He plunged into her like a rabbit on speed, flesh slapping until he yelled out a guttural curse and collapsed on her.

Layla's entire body screamed when she tried

to move Phin off her, but she knew without a doubt that she'd just experienced the best sex of her short life. The men she normally dated would definitely have to up their game to compete with this.

Phin disposed of the condom and wobbled back beside her. She rolled partway to her side and accepted the glass of water he offered.

He looked a little concerned. "Are you okay?"

"Hell, yeah, but I think you've rendered my body inoperable. Good thing this is my bed." She handed him the glass and dropped her head to the cushion. Not that there was anything cushiony about it.

"Come sleep in my bed."

"Unh. Can't move." She heard him shuffling around as he headed to bed. She wanted to follow, but her body wouldn't obey. A chill came over her suddenly, and she realized that she didn't have a blanket. Shit. She had to move. Groaning, she pushed up and stumbled to Phin's bed.

"That didn't take long."

"Got cold."

He flipped back the blanket and she climbed in. Without warning, Phin pulled her close, spooning her, warming and soothing her body.

PHIN WOKE WITH A RAGING HARD-ON, BUT WHEN HE looked at Layla, snuggled into his bed, with a bite mark he'd made on her shoulder, he let her sleep. He jumped into the shower and made a pot of coffee. It had been a long time since he'd had someone spend the night. He discovered he didn't need to be quiet, because Layla slept like the dead. He'd finished two cups of coffee and polished off a couple of doughnuts and she still hadn't stirred.

He thought about his next move. He'd planned to hit a couple of halls today and make some spending money. While he didn't care if Layla stayed in his apartment, he wasn't sure if she'd want to. He had nothing of value, but most people wouldn't be comfortable in a stranger's apartment all day. Then again, they weren't really strangers anymore.

In the bedroom, he set a cup of coffee on the nightstand and jumped on the bed. "Rise and shine, babe."

"Unh."

It was the same sleepy grunt she'd given last night after coming a couple of times. She managed to turn him on without even being conscious. Her head turned against his pillow and she sniffed.

"Coffee?"

"I hope black's okay. The milk is expired and I don't have sugar. Unless you want to scrape some off the doughnuts."

She sat up quickly. "You have doughnuts, too? Man, this is better than a hotel. Coffee in bed delivered by a mostly naked, sexy man and free doughnuts." She stretched across the bed to get the coffee. She inhaled the scent before putting the cup to her lips. "Mmmm ... this is good."

"I'm going to leave in a little bit. You can stay here if you want." He tried to remember if he had a spare key to offer her. Steve probably had one.

"Where are you going?"

"Make some money playing pool." He pulled on a pair of jeans and a T-shirt.

"Can I come?"

Her last word called him back to bed and her naked body, but he fought the urge. He leaned over and kissed her. "You'll be bored."

And I can't afford the distraction.

"I like to watch you play." She shot him a grin as she climbed out from under the covers.

He wanted to tell her no, but found himself slapping her ass. "Get going then. Time is money."

While Layla took a shower, he had another cup of coffee. He'd never had company for a whole day of pool. Part of him cringed at the thought that she'd talk incessantly. The car ride would be bad enough, but what if she talked during the game?

Then again, having her as a distraction would up his game, push him to practice patience.

After a shower and scarfing down a couple of doughnuts, Layla was finally ready to go. Phin tried not to be irritated by her throwing his schedule off, because she took a lot less time than most women he'd come in contact with. Then, one look at her wearing a T-shirt that said "Math Geeks Know All the Angles" written around a tri-angle, and he *couldn't* be mad.

In the truck, Layla fiddled with the radio. He

knocked her hand away. "The dial is temperamental." He turned the knob to a station that came through clearly.

"Like its owner." She sat back and crossed her arms.

"What?"

"You're cranky. Maybe you should've slept in like I did. You could use some beauty sleep."

"I was up late trying to figure out how you cheated at cards last night."

"I didn't cheat. I didn't even use my feminine wiles."

"The hell you didn't. You were barely dressed and, every time you moved, your shirt inched higher, revealing a little more thigh, inviting me over."

She snorted. "Just because you have no self-control does not mean I cheated."

When he came to a red light, he turned to her. She bit her lower lip. She was a horrible liar. He didn't even need to comment for her to break.

"Okay, but it wasn't cheating exactly. Yes, I let my shirt ride up, but that was so you wouldn't pay attention to my face. I learned how to count cards to win at blackjack. I simply improvised and studied what cards were being played so I could win."

"Counting cards doesn't work with gin." He stepped on the gas.

"Technically, no, but I created a method on the fly. I don't know if it really worked. It was kind of like I was trying to memorize the cards laid out and figure out the probability of what you held."

"Good thing you aren't going to Vegas. Use your skills for good not evil."

"Like you do?"

"What do you mean? I taught you how to play pool. That was good."

"You only did that because you wanted to fuck me."

He couldn't argue that.

They sat in silence for a few minutes and then the moment he dreaded hit.

"Tell me about your family of conmen and the rules you balked at."

His grip on the steering wheel tightened. He should've known she'd go there. "What do you want to know?"

"Anything. When someone says the word *con artist* to me, I think about TV and movie characters. Like it would be fun—except the possibility of jailtime part—not something to run away from."

He had no idea where to start. He didn't like to talk about that life. "When I say my family, it was more than the conventional parents and kids. We were more like a commune."

"Like hippies?"

"Sort of. But instead of peace and love and living in one spot, we moved around and supported ourselves by conning anyone who was dumb enough to fall for our tactics." Thankfully, he pulled into the lot for the first pool hall. It was Sunday afternoon, after church, so he hoped to find a few decent games.

"It's got to be kind of exciting though, right?

Moving around all the time. To be totally free from responsibility. It's got to be liberating." She jumped out of the truck before he could even form a response.

Liberating? More like suffocating. He had never had a choice where or when they moved. He had never known if someone would be caught and arrested. That concern had amplified once his mother had left. If his dad were to go jail, Phin had worried about what would happen to him. The family would have taken care of him, but he would've lost the few freedoms that his father had given him.

He got out of the truck with his cue and joined Layla on the other side of the vehicle. She slid an arm around his waist and tugged him close. "One more question and then I'll leave you alone. You obviously hate talking about it."

He looked into her eyes, staring at him so openly and honestly. "Go ahead."

"Why did you leave? It had to have been really hard to walk away."

Phin leaned against his truck, breaking contact with her. He ran his fingers through his hair. "There are certain expectations for each member of the family. I wasn't willing to live up to those expectations."

"Every family has expectations. My family expected me to go to a good college and graduate and then get a decent job. They expect I'll settle down, get married, and give them grandchildren. That's life." She tucked her hands into the pockets of jeans that hugged her slender curves.

"I didn't want to get married."

"Oh."

He shoved off the truck, wanting to leave the subject behind them and focus on the game. True to her word, Layla didn't ask another question, but he knew she was dying to. Leaving his family had been his choice. His mother had made sure he had a taste of a regular life, and a taste was all he'd needed. Now he knew how to find it on his own. Layla was proof of that.

CHAPTER FIVE

*L*ayla walked beside Phin toward the pool hall, thinking about what he'd said. She couldn't wrap her head around it. So what if he didn't want to get married? There had to be more to it. She saw it in his eyes. After he'd stopped talking, she'd watched his countenance change. From trying to hide his wounds to putting on his game face. She wished for half the strength he had.

Phin was the kind of guy to grab life and run with it. He had no fear, whereas for her, there were times when she felt like she was caught in a hurricane of panic. To have complete control of everything . . . Maybe one day she'd feel that way.

They walked through the doors, and Layla looked around. She'd never stepped foot in a pool hall before. She'd known they existed, but she'd always imagined them to be nothing more than a place for motorcycle gangs to hang out—pop culture her only point of reference. Phin studied the layout and chose a table. She took a seat nearby and watched him rack the balls the way she had the previous day when he'd been nothing more than a sexy stranger to look at.

As Phin took his first shot, she eased off her stool and walked to him. "This might be a stupid question, but shouldn't you have asked someone at a different table to play you instead of standing here alone?"

He leaned down and stole a quick kiss. "I'm not alone, babe; I'm with you. And if I wait for someone to come to me, he can only blame himself for losing. I don't look like a predator." He winked and turned back to the table.

She'd watched him play yesterday, and although she'd pegged him as a hustler or a shark easily enough, he didn't look like a predator. He was too friendly, downright charming. He excelled at the role of con man because she'd seen the predator when they were alone together. A bright glimpse in his eye when he knew he'd win.

She hadn't seen it while playing pool or even during gin, but when he'd kissed her and stroked her and then asked if it was okay. That was the predator taking over the con man. Maybe she should've been insulted or even pissed off, but it only made him more intriguing.

Layla had never gone for bad boys. Unlike most girls she knew, she wasn't drawn to the danger. But Phin was a different type of bad boy. She sat back on her stool and watched him clear the table. As he racked the next round, a guy who looked to be about forty sauntered over.

Phin didn't say anything, so the man spoke. "Mind if I play?"

"Sure. I like a little competition. The girl-friend's not really good enough to challenge me."

The man chuckled and heat clawed up Layla's neck. First, Phin had no business calling her his girlfriend, and second, who the fuck was he to say she didn't challenge him? She hopped off her stool and glared at him before heading to the ad-jacent table.

Phin swatted her ass and said in a low voice, "Stay out of trouble."

She slid her money into the table to release the balls. Let him have his game and scam that asshole. She'd play on her own and she'd show him a challenge. After racking the balls, she chose a cue stick and cleared her mind with a deep breath. She tuned out the clacking of balls and the low grumbles of men throughout the hall.

She even managed to ignore Phin's presence and the heady feeling that rose in her every time he looked her way. Single-minded focus was one of her many gifts. She remembered what Phin had taught her about body position and watching where the balls *could* land, not just where they did.

When she reopened her eyes, she leaned over and broke, scattering balls across the table, sinking the three. She circled the table once and studied the balls. Without Phin's interference, she now saw what he'd tried to teach her. In her mind, she imagined the angles and shapes across the table. She leaned over and began her attack. One by one, the solids thunked into pockets.

By the time she sank the last one, she realized she was being watched. Layla glanced over her shoulder and winked at Phin. His opponent was grumbling about losing, but slapped ten bucks on the table. Phin tucked it in his pocket, but his cryptic eyes stayed on her.

"Hey, sweetheart, can I buy you a drink?"

Layla straightened to face the man across from her. "No thanks. I'm good."

"Well, how about a game then? A little friendly wager."

She felt the air shift and knew that Phin had stiffened, but didn't move. "What kind of wager?"

Layla couldn't help but think of her wager with Phin the previous day and all of the delicious things it had led to.

"I win, you let me buy you a drink."

"And if I win?"

"I'll still buy you a drink."

She studied the guy, trying to see him the way Phin would. He stood relaxed, wearing faded jeans and a plaid shirt unbuttoned at the collar. He was tan and his muscles bulged. He worked manual labor of some sort, but that didn't help her determine what kind of player he'd be. But there was Phin burning a hole into her back, so she said, "There's no challenge in that. If I win, you pay me twenty bucks."

"You got it." He placed a twenty on the table.

She dug into her pocket and did the same. He

walked around the table and extended his hand. "I'm Joe."

"Layla." They shook briefly, and Joe turned to rack the balls. "You want to break?"

"Ladies first."

She rolled her shoulders and tried not to be nervous, but closing out all distractions was harder this time. Leaning over, she shot the cue without following through. As soon as the ball rolled, she knew her mistake, but there was no calling it back. There were no do-overs. The white cue ball tapped into the triangle and opened it, but the balls didn't scatter the way they needed to.

Joe made a sound like a lame laugh and said, "We can ditch this game now and go get that drink. It'll relax both of us."

"Your shot," she answered. She took a step back and bumped into Phin. She didn't turn, but knew it was him. God, she so didn't need him laughing at her too. She shifted to get away, but his hand grabbed the back of her waistband.

He lowered his head to her ear. "You can handle this joker. Play like you're alone, like your last game, and you'll wipe the floor with him."

She watched as Joe managed to sink two striped balls before missing. Phin's hand released her jeans, but caressed over her hip as he added, "See it and own it."

Then he was gone. Layla closed her eyes and expelled the anxiety gnawing at her. She went to the table to figure out her options. Her brain took over then. Math never let her down. One by one, she sank every solid. When the eight ball dropped in, Joe groaned.

He picked up his twenty and placed it in her hand. "Good game. I'd still like to buy you that drink."

"No thanks." She watched him walk away and, when she was sure he wasn't going to turn back, she jumped and danced.

"What are you doing?" Phin asked.

"I'm celebrating, of course. Just because winning means nothing to you, doesn't mean I shouldn't get pleasure from it. I won. I can buy dinner tonight." She smiled up at him and then kissed his cheek. "Still think I'm not enough of a challenge for you?"

"You're more challenge than I need in a lifetime. Let's go find some people to play doubles with."

PHIN HAD BEEN A LONE PLAYER HIS WHOLE LIFE. Even when he'd been with his family, he'd struck out alone because that was where he excelled, where he had control. Never had he imagined that hooking up with a partner would be so enjoyable.

In the past, a partner had meant splitting the profits with someone he'd have to carry. Today, with Layla, he'd not only made more money than he had on any other Sunday, but he'd had a great time. They'd laughed and joked and schemed to win. After playing at a couple of pool halls, they'd moved on to a few bars.

When he pulled the stack of cash from his pocket and counted out half to her, her face lit up, but she looked ready to cry.

She giggled uncontrollably while she played with the bills. "Who needs a degree from MIT when I can make this kind of money playing a game?"

He stared at her as he put the key in the ignition. "You can't be serious."

She sobered. "Why would I joke about this much money? I work at the campus bookstore making minimum wage. Do you have any idea how long it would take me to make this much money?"

He turned the key.

"Three days, Phin. And this was fun. Staring at textbooks all day? Not so much."

"We had a good day. It's not always like this. Sometimes I go out and come back with nothing."

"But you still have fun."

He lifted a shoulder. Pool wasn't really about fun for him. It was just a means to an end, unlike when he'd first learned. They picked up a pizza on the way back to his apartment. Layla insisted on paying for it out of her winnings.

At home, Phin popped the tops on a couple of beers while Layla opened the pizza. She'd found an action movie on TV and sat curled on the corner of his couch. It all felt so normal. Like they belonged here together. He shook his head to lose the thought. Layla was passing through the same way he was, and they were headed in opposite directions. She had a life ready and waiting for her. He was still scrambling to figure his out.

He sat next to her and they ate while making fun of the crappy acting in the movie. When the movie ended, they got ready for bed together. Layla had become uncharacteristically quiet. He should ask her what was wrong, but he didn't want to care. Seriousness didn't fit into what they had going. Fun and games until it was time for her to hit the road.

Lying in bed, Phin needed to get them back on track. What better way to have fun than to have sex? Layla hadn't bothered to put on clothes. There was no pretense that they might not have sex. They wanted each other, and playing pool all day, shooting dirty looks across the table, had turned them both on.

She pushed him onto his back and straddled him. The woman liked to think she was in control all the time.

"Hey," she started, and waited to have his full attention.

He stopped groping her breasts and looked at her face.

"I had the best time ever today. Thank you for that."

"Not a problem." He sat up and took a nipple into his mouth.

She pulled away and shoved him back down on the bed. Kissing her way down his neck and then his torso, Layla played with his body. She traced lines along his ribs with her nails, bit at his nipples, and then licked a long trail down his body.

It wasn't until she had gotten to his hip that he realized her intention and jolted up, grabbing her shoulders.

"What?" she asked, startled.

"You don't have to do that."

She wiggled away. "I know I don't have to. I want to."

She moved down his body again and he pulled her up. "No."

Layla laughed. "What do you mean, no? I've never come across a man who didn't want a blow job."

He tossed her off him and sat up. "I don't." He swung his legs over the side of the bed, putting his back to her. He'd never had such a persistent woman before. He'd had other offers, but when he'd relieved them of the expectation, they'd always been more than happy to stop.

But not Layla. Her fingers stroked his back before he felt her breasts pressed to him. "What is it?" she asked softly.

How could he explain? He'd said he had left his family's life behind him, but some things from childhood were imbedded so deep, he didn't know how to let go. "I was taught . . . in our family . . . " There was no way to do this without sounding stupid.

He knew it didn't make sense, but his gut reaction was always the same. It was bad, dirty, impure.

She kissed his shoulder and threaded her fingers into his hair. "Tell me."

"I was raised to believe that anything below the waist was . . . " He sighed. "The only word I've got is impure. We don't wash our shirts or face towels with pants or underwear. After she gives birth, a woman's husband stays away from her in that way."

"That sounds more like a cult than a family." Layla pulled away from his back.

He knew she'd be ready to pack up and go, so he stood. "I know it sounds crazy, but it took me more than a year without my family to do all of my laundry together." And that had been more because he couldn't afford the extra cost.

Her fingers wrapped around his wrist. "Come back to bed."

He sat and then lay, unsure of his next move. Or hers.

Layla stretched her body next to his. She went back to tracing designs on his chest. "I'd like to be your first."

"What?"

"You've never had a blow job, right? And although it was part of your upbringing, it doesn't seem like you really believe it. Let's try." She pushed up against his chest and began kissing his stomach. "If you feel weird, or uncomfortable, we'll stop. You say the word."

He swallowed hard, but there was no spit left in his mouth. His entire head drained, and his heart pumped double-time. Her fingers wrapped around his dick and stroked. He was already hard, so slipping against her palm offered some relief. When he didn't stop her, or tell her no, she moved quickly.

Her tongue ran down the length of him. Wet and warm followed by her cool breath. She shifted her body so she knelt between his legs, giving him full view of his cock being sucked into her mouth. He twitched at the thought, but the sensation felt amazing.

She paused and looked up at him, his tip resting between her lips and teeth, her tongue swirling over it. He nodded, as he pushed down his childhood fears and enjoyed what she offered. She took him in her mouth then and bobbed up and down, creating a rhythm opposite her hand fisted at his base.

He had no words to describe it. Then she pulled away with a loud smacking sound and lowered herself to his balls. She licked and laved her tongue across them and up in between them. Every muscle in his body went taut. Fuck! How had he gone his whole life without knowing this? As his balls began to tighten, Layla brought her lips back to his dick. He grabbed at the sheets, something to hold him together, regain some sense of control.

She began her rhythm again and gently slid her hand to his and placed it on the top of her head. His other hand joined and it felt natural to hold her and guide her as she swallowed him. His tip hit the back of her throat, soft and warm, and his balls were ready to explode.

"Layla. Stop . . . I'm gonna . . ."

"It's okay," she whispered.

"Not that. I . . . can't."

As good as it felt, he couldn't come in her mouth. It didn't feel right. It made him feel like he was demeaning her. She reached across him and grabbed a condom from the nightstand. Before he could gather his thoughts to help her, she had it on him and began riding him. It took only a minute before he came inside her, and it was the most explosive orgasm he'd ever had. He continued to pump until he was empty.

It wasn't until he swallowed that he noticed the rawness of his throat. Had he screamed? Layla climbed off and took care of the condom for him, which was good because he couldn't move. His blood had become lead.

She crawled back into bed and curled next to him. As minutes passed, Phin became able to think again. Layla traced over his skin, but didn't speak until he turned to face her.

"Was it good?"

"Holy fuck was it good. I had no idea how different it would be." He looked down at her wicked little smile and a sudden pang of guilt smacked him. "But it wasn't for you. Shit, I'm sorry. You just moved too fast."

"It's okay." She patted his chest.

He looked at her and wanted her to feel as good as he did. But could he taste her? Lick her? Feel her come apart and control her the way she had him? The idea tempted him, but he had no idea what he was doing. Certainly she wouldn't want to be his first bumbling attempt.

She let out a giggle. "No reciprocation necessary, Phin. I did that because I wanted to, not because I expect the same in return."

He felt relieved, but guilt nagged him. He didn't want to use her for his own pleasure and give nothing. "I think I can reciprocate a little."

"You know, I never expected you to be such a loud lover. Good thing you don't have neighbors."

"Let's see if I can get you to wake the neighborhood."

Then he stroked her and kissed her. He wanted to thank her for changing his outlook and breaking another barrier from his past. He could never give her the words to express it, but he could give her this.

ayla heard noise, but burrowed deeper into the pillows. There was no reason to even consider waking up this early. Sunlight in the room was faint, indicating that no normal human needed to move around. A slap on her bare ass startled her. Pushing the pillow away from her mouth, she groaned. "Go away."

"Give me one minute and then you can go back to unconsciousness."

She rolled over and squinted at Phin. No one should look that good at God knew how early. Even if he was fresh from a shower.

"I put your phone on the charger." He jingled keys in front of her face. Choosing one, he said, "Apartment." Flipping to the other he added, "Truck."

He was giving her keys?

"I'm going to work if you need me. If you go out, be careful."

"You're letting me drive your truck?"

"You'll get bored sitting here all day." He set

the keys on the nightstand. "Don't crash it and don't get robbed."

Now he was a comedian. "Smart-ass." She closed her eyes again, trying to reclaim sleep.

The mattress sank beside her, and Phin's hand ran across her stomach. She eased her eyes open as he lowered his face to hers. "Aren't you going to be late?"

"It takes thirty seconds to get downstairs. I have time for this." He kissed her, making her blood race.

Her hips wiggled and she hoped he'd move his hand lower to touch her. He pulled back and she tried not to moan. A little giggle escaped when she saw him adjusting himself. Nice to know she wasn't the only one who was hot and bothered. "You shouldn't wake someone up like that unless you're gonna follow through."

She rolled over and buried her face in the pillow again.

The bed bounced and Phin was suddenly straddling her backside. "Don't go finishing without me." He curled his hands under her and cupped her smooshed breasts. His warm breath skated across her shoulder and then he nipped her neck.

"What time do you get off?"

"'Bout the same time as you."

She laughed and tried to twist out of his grasp. "I mean when do you get out of work?"

"I know what you meant. Usually around four, but I have extra work on a transmission."

Layla imagined him working on her car, his

talented hands fixing the problem, making everything okay. Phin jumped off her, and she heard him shuffling around, and then the door closed.

She lay on the bed, missing the warmth of his body, the look in his eye when he wanted to fuck, the way he carelessly called her *babe*. How could only two days with a guy seem so real and right? Pulling the covers over herself, she nestled into the scent of Phin around her and went back to sleep.

When she woke hours later, the sun was bright and filled the room. If there had been curtains or blinds on the windows, she probably would've slept for hours more. She scrubbed a hand across her face and into her hair before tossing off the covers and climbing out of bed.

She stumbled to the bathroom to take a shower. Her body ached from all the sex she'd had over the last couple of days, but she felt good—no—satisfied. After her shower, she found Phin's coffee and started a pot. She'd missed a call from Felicity, so she dialed while the coffee brewed.

"Hey, what's up? You in Texas?"

"Yes, I'm here and it's beautiful. Are you going to make it?"

Layla's heart sank. Felicity was counting on her to have a good time. "I don't think so. Phin said it'll take a couple of days to fix my car. Best case, it'll be done on Wednesday. By the time I drive there, it would be time to turn around and head back to school."

The thought of returning to school created an

odd sensation in her gut. Kind of like anxiety amplified. Not school. She'd never had that reaction
to school. School was comfortable and safe. She
always knew what to expect and what to do.

But returning after break was the beginning
of the end. Only weeks until graduation and
starting over.

"No. That's awful. What am I supposed
to do?"

"What do you mean? Have fun. You're capable
of doing this, Felicity. Whenever you're presented
with an opportunity, don't do what you would
normally do. Stop and think 'What would Charlie
and Layla want me to do?' Then do that." She ignored Felicity's groan. "Speaking of Charlie, have
you heard from her?"

"She texted that she was having dinner with
Ethan last night, but she hasn't responded to my
texts today to tell me what happened."

"Wait a minute. You're on spring break and
instead of going out and enjoying yourself, you're
sitting there texting Charlie and calling me?
Leave the hotel room."

"I left earlier."

Layla thought for a minute. "For breakfast,
right?"

Felicity's lack of answer was confirmation.

"Put on your swimsuit, pack a bag, and leave.
Promise me that you won't go back to your room
for at least the next six hours."

"What am I supposed to do for six hours?"

"Swim, sunbathe, drink, pick up a gorgeous
guy, eat, drink some more, make friends."

"That's a lot of stuff I'm not good at."

"Promise."

"I'll try."

"Do or do not. There is no try."

Felicity laughed. "Don't you think it's time to let go of the *Star Wars* quotes?"

"Blasphemer." Layla poured a cup of coffee and sipped, relishing the first jolt of the day. "Go have fun. I plan to."

"I'm sure you do." Felicity's voice held a hint of jealousy. "How did you meet this guy?"

"I met him at a bar. We played pool, and, when my bag went missing, he helped me find it and offered me a place to stay. Plus, he's the mechanic who's working on my car." Layla thought about the many ways she'd lucked out by walking into that bar on Saturday. "He's so much fun, Felicity. We spent the day yesterday playing pool at a bunch of different places. And we made money doing it."

"Isn't that illegal?"

"A friendly game of pool?"

"It's not friendly if there's money involved."

"It's fine. And the sex, oh God, the sex is fabulous. He's rough and gentle and fast and slow and makes my head spin."

"Yeah, I got that part when I called the other night."

Just thinking about having sex with Phin made her horny all over again. "But it's more. He's a good guy. He's strong, and there's a hint of mystery around him. He grew up in this cult-like family of con artists, Felicity. Can you even imagine what living like that would be like? No responsibility other than to your family, traveling around, no regular job. Such a different life."

Until trying to explain it to her friend, Layla hadn't really thought about why she'd been so drawn to Phin and his life. She shouldn't have been, since he seemed to be doing his best to leave that part of himself behind, at least if she went by what he said. From the outside, it still looked like he lived the life of a nomadic con artist. What did he want if it wasn't that life? Why not choose one town, find a regular job, and stay? Plant roots.

Her musings had just given her more questions to ask Phin, and she had no idea if he'd answer them, but she had a deep need to know. She wanted to understand him.

"Are you falling for this guy?"

Falling for him? "I don't know. I've only known him for a couple of days."

"But you're talking like you're all invested in his life. If it was just sex, then that's all you'd be rambling on about. Don't get me wrong, I'm kind of glad you're off that conversation, since I have none coming my way, but you have to know that this can't go anywhere."

Layla inhaled the scent of her coffee before answering. "I'm not doing anything crazy. I'm enjoying my spring break. Phin is not a long-term anything. He's moving on himself soon. Heading to Vegas and who knows where after that." Her mind drifted to another road trip. She'd loved her drive down to Georgia, at least until her car had stopped working. The relaxation of the open road, with the radio up and the windows down, not having to worry about a schedule, had been freeing.

"I really needed a vacation. That's what I'm doing here," she told Felicity. "Spring break. Our last one. I only wish we were together. I found my fling. You need to go get yours. Then we'll talk next week and compare notes."

"I love how you tell me to just 'get one,' as if I've ever been able to do that."

"You can do it. Channel Charlie. That girl will get you laid faster than anything."

"There was a time that was true. Not so since Ethan's been in her life."

They both quieted. They'd spoken before about how they didn't understand what Charlie saw in the man. He was okay, but not the kind of guy they'd ever pictured Charlie with. Layla could actually see Charlie with a guy like Phin. She shook her head. She did *not* need her thoughts going there. "Go hit the beach. I'm going to explore Atlanta. Have fun."

"You too. I'll talk to you later. Give me a call if you need anything."

"Yep." Layla hung up and rummaged through her bag for a new T-shirt. If she was going to spend the rest of her week in Atlanta, she'd have to do laundry. She'd planned on picking up some new clothes in Texas for the week, but now, with no credit card until tomorrow and a repair bill headed her way, the laundromat would be necessary. She piled her dirty clothes up and found a plastic bag to put them in. She'd ask Phin about where to go later. While she polished off her coffee, she scrolled through her e-mails on her phone.

She sputtered on her coffee as she stared at one. Diane Amato. That was the woman she'd interviewed with on Friday. Coffee burned in Layla's stomach and she swallowed hard. Maybe Diane was writing to tell Layla they'd made a mistake. She didn't really have a job offer. Her heart kicked up a notch, and she inhaled slowly before clicking on the message.

> *Dear Layla, I hope this finds you well. I know when we spoke on Friday you said you wanted a week to think about the job offer. I'm assuming you have other leads that you need to explore. I wanted to get you set up in our system should you decide to accept the job. Follow the link below to fill out a complete application.*

Layla stared at the words. Air whooshed from her lungs. An application was simple enough. She just needed a computer and she hadn't seen one in Phin's apartment all weekend. Did he really live without a computer? She stood and walked through the place, as if she couldn't already see everything from her spot on the couch. Nothing inside cabinets, under the bed, or in the sole closet. Maybe he kept it in the truck? That would be silly. If he'd been worried about her stealing it, he surely wouldn't have given her his truck keys.

On her phone she did a search for an Internet café, hoping there would be one close by. She gathered her stuff and Phin's keys and headed out the door. In the garage, a radio blared over the noise of the drills and air pumps and clanking wrenches. The stench of oil filled the air, and Layla tried to block it as she wandered around looking for Phin. She probably could've asked any of the guys wearing blue jumpsuits, but she trusted Phin.

A pair of legs stuck out from beneath a blue minivan. She studied the shoes. They looked like they might be Phin's. "Excuse me?"

"Hey, darlin', is there something I could help you with?" a voice called from behind her.

She turned around. It was the guy who had towed her on Saturday. "Hi, again. I'm looking for Phin."

The sound of wheels rolling near her ankles caught her attention. "You found him."

The tow-truck driver/mechanic shook his head and turned back to the car he was working on. Phin heaved himself up from the floor. "What do you need?"

"A computer. You don't happen to have one, do you?"

"Nope."

"That's what I figured. Can you give me directions here?" She held her phone out to him to see the address of the Internet café. "The GPS on my phone drains the battery too quickly, so I don't want to use it."

Phin wiped his hands on an already greasy rag. "What do you need a computer for?"

"To fill out a job application."

"Planning on staying in Atlanta?" His mouth kicked up into a smile that made her melt.

"Uh . . . no. I interviewed for an internship on Friday and they offered me a job. That's why my friends and I were supposed to celebrate over spring break. I got an e-mail telling me to fill out an online application." She felt silly still holding her phone up to his face when he wasn't even looking at it. His attention was focused on her, so she dropped her arm to her side. "The Internet café is close, I think."

"That'll cost you money you don't have. I'll talk to Steve. He's got a computer in the office he might let you use."

Phin turned and Layla grabbed his arm. "You don't have to do that. You guys have already been really nice. I don't expect any more favors."

"It's a computer. It's not like I'm asking him to give up his lunch." He pulled from her grasp and walked toward the back of the garage.

Layla stood awkwardly flipping her phone over in her hand, feeling out of place in the noise of the garage. Mumbled curses and grunts acted as background to the radio. A couple of guys stood in the corner talking over cups of coffee. One pointed in her direction, making her even more self-conscious.

A shrill whistle sounded from the corner. Phin waved her over. "Steve has errands to run. He said you could use the computer as long as you don't fuck with any of his shit and you're done within an hour."

She hadn't even seen the application yet, so she wasn't sure she could finish in an hour. Even if she didn't, she could start it and figure out what she'd need to finish. If they wanted specifics about her courses, she didn't have that information handy anyway. She followed Phin to a crowded back office. File cabinets filled one wall, and hanging above them were various outdated girly calendars.

Charming.

Layla reminded herself not to be a snot. The guy was doing her a favor. "Thanks," she said as she pulled out the rickety desk chair.

"Need anything else?"

She shook her head, suddenly nervous again.

"I'll be out front if you need me."

She didn't want to need him. Not again. This was the third day she'd done nothing but rely on him. What would she have done if she hadn't met him at the bar? If he had been some other guy? She'd lucked out, and she owed him. The computer was a little on the ancient side, but it was already booted up. She logged on to the Internet and accessed her e-mail to get the link.

The NSA application stared at her. Her fingers flew across the keyboard filling in identification information by rote. Then the questions became more detailed, and she had to actually read them and focus.

She read the questions and felt like a fraud. No matter how she answered, she felt like she was making it up, pretending to know what she was doing. And they would know.

This was the freaking NSA. They would catch her and know she was faking it.

Her hands sat idle on the keys as she read. Looking at all the blank fields was worse than opening a new document before writing a paper. The boxes and spaces indicated how much she needed to do. The tingle started at the top of her spine and shot across her skull.

No! She had no reason to panic. It was a stupid application. Words on a page. She'd done the work, had the knowledge. She just needed to share it.

But the familiar ropes wrapped themselves around her chest, and her breaths became shallow. She pushed away from the desk and closed her eyes. Her panting echoed loudly in the room, and sweat broke out from every pore.

She needed to get out. The office had no windows so she couldn't even pretend to grab fresh air. Glancing at the computer, she hit the exit button.

Do you want to save before exiting? If you do not, all information will be lost.

The message glared at her and she pressed no. No, she didn't want to save any information that would cause a panic attack. She shoved away from the desk on stiff legs. Tears threatened and her throat burned. Outside the office door, she looked back the way Phin had brought her in.

She couldn't go that way. The room full of men would stare; the noise would make the panic claw harder. *Phin.* She didn't want Phin to see her broken like this. To the right was another door, one she hoped led outside. She slammed her body against the metal and walked out into the bright sun.

The glare caused the tears to spill over, but a breeze swirled around her. She opened her mouth as if to catch the moving air. She knew better. Knew she needed slow, deep breaths, but gulping the fresh air and sunshine was what her body craved. Before she knew it, she was light-headed. She sank to her knees, loose asphalt and rough concrete digging through her jeans.

She bowed her head and finally slowed her breathing and her heart. The sun beat on the back of her neck, keeping her warm, while the breeze cooled and dried the sweat on her arms.

The last wave left her spent. She wanted to move. Needed to, really, but she wasn't sure her body would cooperate. A few more deep breaths and she shoved up from the ground on wobbly legs. Her muscles ached.

Why did she always forget that part?

Whenever she thought about a panic attack, she remembered the shortness of breath, the feeling of being trapped, the funky sweat, but she always forgot how her muscles ached after.

Layla ran her hands over her face to wipe away the remaining tears and then inched forward slowly. She needed to find a way to get back to Phin's apartment with no one noticing. She edged around the building on the back side. Looking up, she could see his apartment, but a rusted fence stood in her way. She knew she'd have to pass the open bay doors and risk Phin's seeing her if she went around the front, so she'd hop the fence.

Anything to avoid someone seeing her like this.

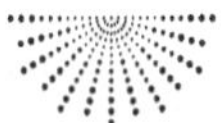

*P*hin peeled back the top of his jumpsuit and let it hang on his hips. His stomach was growling something fierce and he needed food. He checked Steve's office to ask Layla if she wanted to eat, but the office was empty. His stomach grumbled again. The truck was still where he'd parked it last night, so Layla was around somewhere.

He hadn't seen her leave and, with the way the other guys had been ribbing him since she came in, he knew they would've said something if they'd seen her when she was on her way out. He walked around the garage to his apartment. There wasn't much food at his place, so Layla had to be at least as hungry as he was.

Inside the apartment, he was surprised to find Layla curled up in a ball on his couch wearing just a T-shirt and panties. Was she sick? She'd looked fine when she came down before. He sat on the edge of the cushion and nudged her. "Are you okay?"

She rolled over and without opening her eyes, grumbled, "Hey, what's up?"

"Not you. Are you sick or something?"

She sat up rubbing her eyes. When she finally looked at him, he realized that she'd been crying.

"No, I just got tired, so I lay down to take a nap. I thought you had to work late."

He realized that she wasn't going to mention why she'd been crying. "I do, but I'm on lunch. Want to go grab something?"

A smile eased across her face. "Mmmm . . . sounds good. I'm really hungry."

She twisted to get off the couch and knocked Phin off in the process. His ass landed on the floor with a thump. He should've seen it coming, but he'd been distracted by her smile and how much he wanted to kiss her. Now that mouth was laughing at him.

Layla bit her lip to stop the laughter and stood over him, arm extended to help him up. "Sorry."

He grabbed her hand and pulled her down on top of him. She landed with an *oomph* of surprise. He enjoyed the feel of her soft body against his and debated how important it was to go back to work. She licked her lips. The sight of her pink tongue had his dick twitching, as he remembered the pleasure she'd given him last night.

Then she lowered her lips to his and kissed him as if she knew exactly where his thoughts had gone. Like the rest of her body, her lips were soft and sleepy and warm. It made him want to crawl into bed with her and spend the rest of the day there. She wiggled against his hard dick and deepened the kiss. The woman drove him crazy.

He gripped her hips and rolled her beneath him, smacking his head on the table in the process. He shoved the table out of the way and pulled her shirt up. No bra. He knew he liked this girl. Phin pulled an erect nipple into his mouth and she arched against him.

Food was overrated.

He feasted on Layla, licking and sucking her skin until she was moaning and bucking beneath him. They both fumbled at snaps and zippers to be able to feel skin on skin. While he peeled away more of the jumpsuit and the jeans underneath, Layla reached into her backpack, returning with a condom. She sat with the condom in her hand waiting for him to spring free.

She had him covered and was pulling him back down on top of her faster than he could register it. Her panties lay next to her. She wrapped her legs around his hips and guided him in. "I'm ready now, Phin," she whispered.

He drove into her, but held still for a minute to experience the warm, wet comfort.

She dug her heels into him. "Faster."

He took her command to heart and thrust into her. She gripped the leg of the couch to anchor herself from sliding across the floor. The room was filled with their rapid breathing and the slick sounds of sex. Phin rose up and hooked an elbow under her knee to drive deeper.

Her eyes remained on him, so intent that he almost lost his rhythm. With his other hand he reached for her clit and pressed his thumb against it, causing pressure with each thrust. He felt her tightening, watched her knuckles go white against the leg of the couch as she wrapped her other hand on his forearm. Her nails dug into his skin. Her breath came in quick pants until she shattered, still staring deep into his eyes.

Once her muscles pulled him deeper, he leaned back over her, bracing his elbows on the floor, and quickened the pace. She felt so damn good that he didn't want this to end, but he needed to finish, needed to feel her wrapped around him again, needed more.

Layla folded her arms and legs around him and held on while he pounded into her until he went blind. Then there was nothing.

He couldn't see, couldn't hear, except for the blood roaring in his ears. But he could feel. Layla's fingers ran a lazy trail down his back, down and then back up to play with his ponytail. He concentrated on the play of her hands until his other senses came back online. Finally able to move again, he pulled out of her with a loud sucking sound, but stayed in her arms for another minute. "Shit, if you're gonna kill me, that's the way to go."

She laughed again, loud and unrestrained. He eased off her and saw no signs of the girl who had been crying, and he was glad he could do that much for her. He staggered to the bathroom to clean up. He retied his hair and slipped back into his jumpsuit. So much for lunch. He walked back into the living room and saw Layla still lying on her back, splayed naked on his floor. She was such a fucking beautiful sight. What he wouldn't give to come home to that every night.

Whoa! Where the fuck had that come from?

He walked past her, averting his eyes so he wouldn't be tempted to get naked again. He needed to get back to work. To fix her transmission so she could go home.

She wouldn't be here more than another day or two. He needed to accept that. Moreover, he needed to get his libido to accept that. Phin nabbed the last semi-stale doughnut from the box.

"Hey, I thought we were getting lunch."

"Lunch is over. Back to work." He looked at her lying there, totally comfortable with his staring. He cleared his throat and almost choked on some powdered sugar. "Remember where the burger place is up the street?"

She nodded slowly with a sly smile on her face. She knew exactly what she was doing to him and she was getting off on it. "I'll pick up some food and bring it back to you," she said.

"Don't worry about me."

"You need to be able to keep your strength up." Her smile widened and her tongue darted out.

He swallowed a groan. "I'll be done in a few hours. I'm starting on your car now."

She shoved off the floor, resigned that he wasn't going to rejoin her. "Have a good afternoon at work." She wiggled her fingers at him over her shoulder as she headed to the bathroom.

The afternoon would be sweet torture. He'd get lost in thoughts of what they'd just done, yet be tormented by the idea that she was so close but they couldn't do it again until he finished work for the day. She might be the death of him.

Forty-five minutes later, Phin felt something shift, and he knew Layla must've come into the garage. The guys stopped working, just like they had earlier in the day. Like they'd never seen a pretty chick before. He turned around to see her just standing there, waiting.

She smiled and held up the bag she had in her hand. "I brought you lunch."

Fuck, yeah. Although the sex had been great, the doughnut had barely taken the edge off his hunger. He tilted his head toward the table in the back. He let her lead so he could shoot dirty looks at his coworkers. They responded with lewd gestures.

If they only knew . . .

Layla pulled burgers from the bag and set them on napkins. He dragged a stool over so she could sit. He remained on his feet and bit into the burger before he even had the wrapper all the way off.

Her cheeks pinked and she said, "Sorry I ruined your lunch break."

He wiped a hand across his mouth. "Never apologize for great sex. I'm just really hungry." He drank from the Coke she set in front of him. "So how did the application go? You scooted out of here without my seeing."

She played with the wax paper around her

burger and averted her eyes. "It's fine. I'll finish it some other time."

"What's wrong? You were upset when I woke you up at lunch." Suddenly, he thought of the other mechanics and the way they looked at her. "Did one of those assholes do something to you?"

"Who?"

He hitched a thumb over his shoulder.

She shook her head. "No. They don't even notice me."

He snorted. "So what was it then?"

"I don't want to talk about it."

He ate some more. "Doesn't seem fair that you keep prying into my life but you won't answer a simple question."

"Maybe later."

He crumpled the wrapper and shoved it back in the bag. After cramming a few fries into his mouth, he said, "Gotta get back. Thanks for lunch."

She shrugged. "No problem. Want to go play pool after work?"

For someone who hadn't played at all up until a few days ago, she seemed way too interested. "Sure. After dinner."

He turned and went back to work, wondering what secrets Layla was keeping.

~

FOR THE NEXT THREE DAYS, LAYLA WAS RELAXED and calm. She hadn't felt the slightest hint of a panic attack. Life in Georgia was better than she'd thought possible considering she was broke and her car was in the shop.

But things had turned for her. She and Phin fell into a routine. She went grocery shopping so they could eat lunch together and still have time for a quickie. He worked; she did their laundry. It felt very homey. More comfortable than she'd felt in a long time. The thought of going back to school and then on to a job with the NSA was starting to lose its appeal.

Phin had the right idea—float around and enjoy life.

She felt free with Phin. She didn't have to pretend or … She could just be herself.

When he walked in from work Thursday evening, he set her car keys on the counter. "You're all set. Car's fixed. You can head out whenever you're ready."

She stared at the keys for a minute and tried to decipher what he was saying. Did he want her to leave? His voice revealed nothing. He'd given no indication that he wanted her gone. In fact, he'd done just the opposite, including her in everything he did. She didn't believe he'd done that out of some sense of courtesy.

"What if I'm not ready?"

He froze on his trek to the bathroom for his shower. "You want to stay? I thought you had plans in Texas."

"Spring break is almost over. By the time I drive there, I'll have to turn around. Besides, I'm having a pretty good spring break right here." She swallowed and added what she didn't want to say.

"But I totally get it if you want me to leave. I've been all up in your stuff for days now. I don't want to overstay my welcome."

He turned and took the few steps back to where she stood. "I'm having a damn fine time myself." He lowered his head and kissed her without touching her with his greasy hands. No part of them connected other than their lips.

How he managed to convey so much with just a kiss startled her. He wanted her to stay. Giddiness rose in her chest. The feeling was such a welcome sensation compared to the pressure she'd been feeling.

Phin pulled away. "I'm going to shower."

She was going to stay with Phin.

While Phin cleaned up, Layla grabbed the newspaper she'd picked up earlier. She scanned the classifieds for a job. She knew it wouldn't be anything special, but neither was her job at the bookstore. And that managed to pay the bills. She couldn't in good conscience keep letting Phin pay for everything.

Well, she had chipped in for food and gas with her winnings from pool. Plus, if she brought in some more money, it would make the trip to Vegas that much easier. All she needed was a simple, mindless job to bring in cash. She circled a few prospects and folded the paper. Tonight, they'd celebrate. Tomorrow, she'd go out to fill out applications.

The thought of applications brought her back to the NSA. She'd have to get back to them and decline the job, but she couldn't think about that yet. At least not without getting all twisted up inside. Maybe she just needed a break. There were only a couple of months left to the school year. If she didn't go back, it would be stupid, but she could take some time, a couple of extra weeks to figure it out. Worst case, she could take incompletes in her classes and finish later. She had until at least Monday to get back to the NSA. By then, she'd be settled here, with Phin.

Then she'd have to break the news to her parents. They wouldn't be happy, but lots of people took time away from life, right? She'd always heard about people trying to find themselves. This was her chance to live her life and find out who she really was.

She went to the bedroom to change before going out. She slipped into the new silk panties she'd splurged on. Phin hadn't seen them yet, so she'd take pleasure in whispering in his ear tonight, letting him know what she wore and letting his mind wander.

Everything was uncomplicated between them. She hadn't known how much a simple life would make her feel at ease.

~

FOR THE LIFE OF HIM, PHIN COULDN'T FIGURE OUT how his life had taken such a turn. He'd finished Layla's car on Wednesday, but he hadn't told her. He liked having her around, and he wanted to put off her leaving. But then Steve had pointed out that he wanted to get paid, so Phin gave Layla her keys.

He hadn't expected her to want to stay.

Sure, he knew they were having a great time, but she had plans. Plans that didn't include him. He didn't know what he was going to do next week when she really was gone. Over the last few days, every time she spoke about her life, he'd tried to envision himself as part of it. Her family and friends had become such vivid images in his mind that he believed that if he were to run into them on the street, he'd recognize them.

He wanted to crawl inside her life and plant himself there. She had everything he'd been working toward: a family, a home, real friends who called even when they weren't near, and roots. Connections to places that had meaning.

Phin had never experienced that, and Layla refreshed that longing in him. He'd checked his bank balance and determined that Vegas would be his last tournament. He had money to start his new life. The question was: *Where* was that life?

Layla stirred next to him, her smooth skin gliding along the length of his body. He'd definitely miss this. She stretched and released her usual morning groan, but then she sat up. She never got out of bed before him. He eased away from her, knowing that he only had maybe another night or two with her in his arms.

Longing gripped him, and he pushed it aside so he wouldn't ruin their last couple of days together.

"What are your plans for today?" he asked.

"I'm filling out job applications." She stood at the foot of the bed and pulled on her clothes.

"Need Steve's computer again?"

"Nope. I've got a couple of places where I can walk in and apply."

Phin's brain fogged. Walk? Where?

Oblivious to his confusion, she went to the bathroom and brushed her teeth and fixed her hair. When she came out she asked, "Meet at the bar for pool tonight? I'm feeling lucky."

"First, pool is never about luck. Second, where are you filling out applications?"

"There are a couple of shops not too far from here. Minimum wage, but it should be enough, given what we make at pool."

He stared at her and tried to understand. She spoke English, but nothing made sense. "Why are you filling out applications here?"

She shrugged. "I can't let you keep footing the bill. I do my share."

"What about school?"

Layla froze, eyes widening like she'd been zapped. "I'm not going back. I'm taking a break. You said you were having fun too."

A new feeling rose in his chest, but he couldn't name it. "What's your plan?"

"Stay here until you're ready for Vegas, and if things are still good between us, I'll follow you."

"You'll follow me?" It had been so long since he'd had someone want to be with him, to stick it out, that he wasn't sure how to respond. Thoughts spun dizzily in his head. He couldn't be responsible for her.

She wrapped her arms around him. "No pressure. I'll take off if you want me to . . . but I want you to know how much this week has meant to me. I've been free with you, and I don't want to lose that." Her body pressed against his, and he held her for long minutes, processing what she'd said.

Then she pulled away and planted a kiss on his cheek. "We'll talk more over dinner. See you at the bar?"

He nodded numbly. After she scooped up her keys and left, it finally hit him that she was going to walk away from a life that held everything he'd ever wanted in order to be with him. Or at least what she believed she got from him.

She had no idea what she was doing.

How was she supposed to fit into his life on the road? He couldn't even focus on a plan for himself. How could he worry about her too?

Phin went to work, trying to figure out how to convince Layla that his life was not one she really wanted. As much as he wanted her in his life—no, as much as he wanted to be in her life—he couldn't let her give up everything.

A surge of excitement energized Layla as she drove toward the bar. She was early, and knew Phin wouldn't get there for a while yet, so she'd practice without him. Maybe have a celebratory beer because she had landed a job. It was still a bookstore, but at least this one was a regular place, so she wouldn't have to look at textbooks all day.

She parked in front of the bar and saw Phin's truck a few spaces in front of hers. She couldn't deny the tingle that skittered up her spine at the thought of his being there, waiting for her. Sharing a beer with him to celebrate would be that much sweeter. Layla jumped from her car and rushed into the bar to find Phin. She knew he'd be by the tables; it was the only place he'd be.

When she got to the back of the bar, she pulled up short. Phin was there all right, leaning against a pool table with some other woman standing between his legs as he kissed her. Layla stared, unmoving, with her knees and her lungs locked. Rage boiled up in her stomach and the fury needed an outlet.

Tears pricked at her eyes as she forced air into her lungs and looked around for a weapon. A tall glass of beer sat on a nearby table, unguarded. She grabbed the glass and threw the contents over Phin and the woman

That got their attention. The woman sputtered and squealed. "What the fuck?"

"My sentiments exactly." Layla eyed Phin. "I thought we were partners."

Phin shrugged. "You're not a good enough player to be my *partner*."

Although he didn't move, he at least had to decency to look away. But he didn't look surprised. He'd expected her to come here. He'd wanted her to witness this. That made her anger run hotter. As she took a step toward him, the woman backed away, obviously wanting to get out of Layla's line of fire.

Layla poked Phin's chest. "If you didn't want me, all you had to do was say so." She ignored the tightness in her chest and continued. "You're the one who's not good enough."

Without waiting for a response, she spun on her heel and left. As she sat behind the steering wheel of her car, tears streamed down her cheeks. Sorrow, anger, resentment, hurt. She let the tears flow, not knowing which emotion to hold on to. When she finally started the engine, she'd decided that no one, least of all Phin, would tell her that she wasn't good enough.

PHIN ROLLED OVER, OR AT LEAST ATTEMPTED TO, and smacked his knee on the steering wheel. He cracked his bleary eyes open and tried to remember . . . anything. His head thumped as he sat up, and his stomach threatened to heave. He leaned his head against the headrest as memories flooded his brain.

He'd left work early to start drinking because he'd known he couldn't tell Layla to go back home if he were sober. Then the perfect opportunity had presented itself in the form of Katie. He and Katie had hooked up a couple of times when he'd first started working for Steve. Letting her come on to him had made chasing Layla off easier.

Fuck. Nothing had been easy last night. He couldn't stand that he'd hurt Layla, but he'd known she'd never listen to him. She was right; he wasn't good enough for her. He couldn't give her what she was used to. And no matter what she told herself, she would want that again.

Starting the truck, he tried to focus on the street ahead of him. The short drive back to his apartment was painful on many levels. Walking in the door and noticing the lack of any sign of Layla almost floored him. He grabbed his bags and started packing. No way could he stay here. He'd lived in this apartment for months and, in the matter of a week, Layla had turned it into their place.

Guilt and loneliness battled for space in his chest. He collected the last of his pay from a grumpy Steve and climbed back in his truck. Images of Layla, hurt and teary-eyed, chased him out of town.

Without Layla, he'd be able to refocus on his goals. He was on track to get everything he wanted.

He managed to get outside Atlanta before pulling over to sleep off the rest of his hangover and erase Layla from his memory.

CHAPTER 8

*L*ayla stood at the counter waiting to receive her registration materials. She halfway listened to the guy behind the counter ramble on about practice hours and dress codes. There was a dress code for a pool tournament? She smiled and accepted the packet. She'd already checked into her room, so she stood off to the side to check out the competition while reading through the schedule.

If only she could figure out which of these people were amateurs and which were pros. Then she snickered at herself. She knew she was really looking for Phin. They hadn't been in contact at all since that night at the bar, so she didn't know if his plans had changed. And really it didn't matter.

She'd decided to participate in the tournament more for herself than for Phin. Having him witness how good she'd become would just be a bonus.

The petty part of her wanted to rub it in his

face. Not only was she good enough to play, but she was good enough to beat him.

She'd spent that weekend on her drive back to school crying and miserable. Talking to Felicity hadn't helped. She'd managed to completely fall in love. At least Layla could commiserate with Charlie. They'd both come out of spring break hurting.

After returning to school, Layla had accepted the job with the NSA and poured herself back into her classes. She used every spare moment learning to be a better pool player, including playing in small tournaments. That intense focus had soothed her heart and kept the panic at bay.

Pushing herself to be in control, to be better, was the best medicine for her anxiety. Graduation came and went, and her new job started in two weeks. The timing was perfect.

A few players walked by and looked at her, but said nothing. Many of them seemed to know each other. She heard greetings all throughout the hall. Maybe the world of pool was small. She could ask if Phin was there. Or she could wait for the pairings to be listed. Tomorrow morning would come soon enough.

She shoved her papers into her bag and headed to the practice area. The banquet hall had been transformed into a huge pool hall. For all the smacking of balls, the silence between opponents screamed. Noticing the way everyone was dressed, she scanned her memory for directions. Had the guy said there was a dress code for the practice area? She glanced down at her T-shirt and jeans. They were clean and respectable.

Moving down the length of the hall, Layla kept her eyes on the tables. People were here to win. It wasn't like playing in a bar for twenty bucks. These players used practice as a means to assess the competition before actual play. She saw it on their faces, calculating who they thought they could beat.

She knew better than to tip her hand. She wouldn't let them test her confidence. It would be her luck to get into a game with a pro and not realize it until he tromped all over her. No. Better not to practice here. She checked her watch. If she had a quick bite to eat in her room, she could find a local bar to practice at and still get a good night's sleep.

Plus, she wouldn't have to worry about running into Phin if he was here.

An hour later, the sun sat burning low in the sky as she stepped out of a cab. After she'd flirted with the concierge, he had recommended this bar and assured her not only that had he not referred any other player there, but that it was clean and friendly.

The noise of the bar put her at ease. If only she could pipe these sounds into the competition hall. She grabbed a beer and walked around to find a pool table. When she reached the back of the bar, her heart jumped into her throat. A man leaned over the table to take a shot. Although she couldn't see his face, she knew that ass. Her body responded before her brain. By the time her brain

told her to back out of the room, he had straightened and turned as if someone had called his
name.

Phin.

Had she said it out loud?

He stared at her, and the first thing she noticed was that he'd cut his hair. It was close-
cropped and highlighted his eyes more than ever.
But she still couldn't read them.

Layla swallowed hard and forced a smile.
She'd known this was a possibility. Well, not here,
but she'd known his plan. She'd done what she
could to prepare for it, but it hadn't been nearly
enough.

She was strong and wouldn't let him get to
her. He needed to know that too, so she took a
couple of steps. She channeled her inner ice
queen, but it didn't feel right with Phin. "Hi,
Phin."

His mouth opened and closed. Phin, man of
few words, was speechless. Big surprise.

He stepped forward and raised his hand to
touch her and then let it drop. "Layla."

He spoke her name as if he needed to hear it
to know it was her. She just nodded.

"What are you doing here?"

"I'm in the tournament. After listening to you
talk about the purse on this one tournament, I
couldn't pass it up."

He continued to stare at her, and she knew he
wasn't listening to her at all. She remembered
the feeling of being taken in by the mere sight of
a person. But she couldn't understand his reac-

tion when he was the one who had pushed her away.

"How have you been?"

"Good. I finished school, landed a great job that I start in a couple of weeks, and spent time prepping for the tournament." She took a sip from her beer more to wet her throat than because she was thirsty. Who knew how hard it could be to act cool? "Are you going to stare all night, or are we going to play?"

She didn't know if he'd remember their first conversation, and thought repeating his first words to her would sound sarcastic, but a shadow crossed his eyes.

"Can we talk?" His question was quiet and intimate. His presence pulled her in, but she fought it.

Walking past him, she said, "I'm not here to talk. I want to practice. I'll rack."

ALL OF THE AIR HAD BEEN SUCKED OUT OF THE room. Phin waited to watch people drop dead. He glanced around and realized he was the only one struggling for breath.

Never.

That's exactly when he thought he'd see Layla again. Except on his computer. After he hit the road, he sank some of his money into a cheap laptop just so he could check up on her. He knew she had graduated and gotten a job, but he'd had no idea she'd planned on joining the tournament.

Layla was here. Acting cool as anything. He didn't like this side of her. He liked her hot and frenzied, angry, or laughing. Anything but indifferent. He turned toward the table, forcing air into his lungs. He wouldn't let her stay distant. If she hated him, he could understand, but to act like they'd never had something special was a different situation. That was unacceptable.

She had the balls racked and her beer sat on the table behind her. She wanted to play; he'd give her a game. He shot her a smile. "I'll break."

One shoulder lifted as if it didn't matter, and she went back to her beer. He made his first shot, sinking nothing. He couldn't remember the last time he broke without sinking a single ball. Months later and Layla was still fucking with his head. He couldn't let her get to him. Not for this tournament.

Layla grabbed a pool cue and walked the table. Phin read her shirt. **Computers allow you to make mistakes faster than anything else. With the exception of a handgun or tequila.**

"No math shirt?"

"Double major, remember?" She leaned over the table and lined up her shot.

"Tequila. I'll keep that in mind when I want you to make a mistake."

She paused and looked up at him. "I'm finished with those kinds of mistakes."

"We'll see."

She struck and sent the four into the side pocket. She walked the table and called her shots. Phin barely focused on the table. Layla had gotten worlds better. Competitive didn't begin to describe this kind of determination. When it was his turn, he half-assed it, wanting to see her work the table.

"Look, if you're not going to really play, get away from the table. I'm here to win."

"I thought pool was fun."

"Things change."

He studied her face, searching for proof of what he wanted to see, that she still cared about him. Yeah, things changed, but everything couldn't just disappear, could it? Then an idea struck. "Fine. What are we playing for?"

She reached into her pocket and slapped a twenty on the table.

"I don't want your money."

She flinched and he saw the pulse at her neck quicken, her throat work as she swallowed. He wanted his mouth on that spot.

"What do you want?"

"A kiss. I win, I get to kiss you."

She snorted. "No way."

"What's the big deal? If you're over me, a kiss shouldn't matter."

Her spine stiffened. Oh, yeah, she was determined. "Fine. What do I get if I win?"

"I'll let you take me back to the hotel and have your way with me."

"Been there, done that, burned the T-shirt."

Phin took a step closer. She wavered, but didn't step back. Stubborn thing, his Layla. He froze. *His* Layla? "What do you want?"

She narrowed her eyes. "Nothing."

He leaned forward and whispered in her ear. "I'll go down on you."

He pulled away in time to see her cheeks flush. She raised one eyebrow.

"I'll stay fully dressed. It'll be all about you."

Her chest heaved and he was almost close enough for it to brush him. What he wouldn't give to feel her pressed against him.

"Given your lack of experience, that might not be doing much for me."

He stepped back with a hand over his heart. "You wound me. Like you, I'm a fast learner. I can pretty much guarantee it would do plenty for you."

"A drink," she said hoarsely. She turned and took a gulp of beer. "You can buy me a drink."

He flashed her a smile. The cold barrier she'd walked in with was crumbling, and that was all he needed to see. If she hated him, he'd have to live with it, but she didn't. He had another shot with Layla, and he wasn't about to let this one slip by.

What the fuck am I thinking?

She circled the table and attempted a shot but only managed to move the balls around.

All the pool practice in the world couldn't have prepared her for coming face-to-face with Phin. Playing pool with him wasn't a problem, but his flirting might kill her. She still wanted him and she hated herself a little for it. She watched nervously as his demeanor changed. He went from happy-go-lucky to pool shark in two seconds flat.

This wasn't just any old game to him.

Unfortunately, she didn't know what to make of it. She hadn't come to Vegas to find him. At least that's what she kept telling herself. The nagging voice in the back of her head disagreed.

Okay, yeah, she had wanted to find him, but it was just to show him that she was good enough, that they could've been partners.

But now, none of that seemed to matter. He acted like he hadn't crushed her two months ago. Like he could pick up right where they'd left off.

He sank three balls and sent her a smirk. Her heart sank with the next ball.

This wasn't Phin wanting to pick up again. He was playing her. The con man in him was stronger than even he suspected. He was worried that she'd screw up his game for the tournament.

Confusion swirled in her chest again. Part of her was relieved, but the other part dredged up the pain of losing him. She didn't want to care about him, didn't want to feel anything when he looked at her.

But she did.

Layla never even got another chance at the table. Phin cleared it with determination. Enough was enough. First he played a crappy game to amuse himself, and then he played to crush her again. And he claimed not to be a hustler.

"Thanks for the game." She set her cue down and finished her beer.

He rounded the table and talked toward her. "Planning on welching on our bet?"

The way he said it irked her, like she routinely didn't pay up. He stood in front of her, and the air surrounding them crackled. She was sure if they touched, the shock would send her heart into spasms. She rolled her eyes, as if the bet were childish, which in a way it was. She didn't know what he thought it would prove, but she puckered up.

He smirked again as his hand settled on her hip. No shock, but warm pulses shot through her, gaining momentum and converging between her legs.

"I know we were only together for a week, but have I ever kissed you like I would kiss a grandma?"

"You didn't stipulate what kind of kiss. A grandma kiss is about all you deserve." She ignored the heat pooling in places where she craved his touch.

He pulled her hips to him and said, "I'm going to kiss you now."

He lowered his head and Layla tried to focus. She did. She wanted to keep the kiss impersonal, but nothing with Phin was ever distant. The moment his lips touched hers, she lost her fragile grasp on her plan.

Kissing Phin was like coming home after her first semester at college. Comfortable and exciting because she'd become a different person.

His tongue swept into her mouth and she moaned. She hadn't kissed anyone since leaving

Atlanta, but even if she had, she knew it wouldn't top this.

Phin pushed her against the table. The wood bit into her backside as he changed the angle of his kiss to go deeper, take more from her.

And he almost had her. She almost gave in and gave him whatever he wanted, but she shoved him off. They stared at each other for a long moment, chests heaving, eyes hazy with lust. He was hard everywhere and she wanted to climb all over him, but instead she wiped her hand across her tender lips. As if she had any chance of removing the impression he'd made.

Then his expression softened. He touched her cheek. "Layla—"

She slapped her hand on his chest. "Don't. You got your kiss."

"That chick in Atlanta didn't mean anything. You know that."

Layla sidestepped him. "I do know. You wanted to get rid of me and used her to do it because you never have the balls to just talk. To open up and let someone see what you need. I got the message. Good-bye, Phin."

"Let me talk now."

"There's nothing you can say. I wouldn't believe you. Can't you see that? You couldn't even play a fair game with me here. You fucked around and then hustled me when you thought you had something to gain. I know I deserve better than that." She walked away, fighting every instinct she had to turn around and give him that chance he asked for.

She tasted him on her lips, and the phantom presence of his body clung to her skin. Two months had not been nearly enough time to get over him. Nothing could be done about that now, though, so she would just refocus and win the games ahead.

$\mathcal{P}$hin entered the tournament hall to scope out the competition and find Layla. He wanted to talk to her. The schedule said she'd be playing now. Part of him hoped she'd lose. He didn't want to play against her in the tournament. He'd have to let her win, and, if that happened, he'd need to find another tournament with a similar purse.

It didn't take long to find her. The number of women playing was still small enough that they stood out in the crowd. He edged closer as her opponent took a shot. The guy missed, mostly because he was staring at Layla's cleavage. She looked over her shoulder and caught his attention with a smile.

He'd been sure she was pissed. Maybe he was wrong. Then she bent over and took her turn. Again and again until she won. Her opponent barely congratulated her.

When she approached Phin, he said, "Good game. You've gotten better."

"Go big or go home, right?"

"That's one way to play it."

"It's still the only way."

The conversation brought him back to their first night together. He wished he could go back to fix something, anything. He watched her walk away from him again, this time with a little swagger. He waited in the hall until his turn to play and he won, as expected. He'd learned over the years that the opening rounds went quickly with the players who were true amateurs being knocked out. The best quickly rose to the top. Layla had become part of that group. He made plans with some of the regular players to meet up in the practice hall.

The practice area was mostly empty when they arrived. Of course, Layla was there. He wondered how many hours she'd clocked playing pool over the past couple of months to be able to excel the way she had.

One of the guys, Jim, elbowed Phin and pointed to Layla. "Hot piece of ass. What do you think? Pool groupie?"

Phin had heard of pool groupies before, but he'd always been too focused on the game to pay any real attention. Hearing the other player talk about Layla like that annoyed the shit of him. He looked at Jim. "More like piranha."

"You know her?"

"Yeah."

Jim led the group to Layla's table. "Hey, I'm Jim. Want to play doubles?"

Layla's gaze took in Jim and then moved on to

the rest of them, landing on Phin. A smile joined the slight shake of her head. "Why not? Layla," she added.

Jim sidled up to her. "Me and Layla against Greg and Phin," he said by way of introduction.

"I was thinking it would be a better game if Layla and I teamed up. We both know I'm the better player. You can't afford the handicap," Phin answered.

She snorted behind Jim, but didn't argue. Jim racked the balls and Phin went to Layla.

She stared at him with narrowed eyes. "Handicap?" she whispered.

"These guys are arrogant assholes just looking to sleep with you. You know me; I play to win."

Her eyes went from slits to saucers. He loved to surprise her. Phin approached the table knowing that he would do everything in his power to set Layla up with every possible shot so she could stomp these two. He had nothing against Jim and Greg. They ran into each other a few times a year at tournaments. They had never become friends, but Phin didn't make friends with anyone.

Not until Layla. And look how that had turned out.

They played in silence, except for a few jeering comments from Jim. If he ever had a shot with Layla, it disappeared as soon as he ran his mouth.

Phin and Layla communicated without words. A sly look, a bump of shoulders . . . He stopped himself before he slapped her ass. After winning two games back to back, Layla took apart her cue. "Thanks for the games, boys, but I'm done. I want to see the rankings for tomorrow and head out."

"How about dinner?" Jim asked.

"No thanks." She turned and headed to the door.

Phin couldn't watch her leave again. She was getting too good at it. "Hey," he said when he caught up.

"Hey."

"You really kicked ass back there."

"You weren't so bad either." She kept walking toward the elevator as if the conversation was pointless. Or maybe it was just him.

Every time he thought he'd made some progress, she cooled off. "Do you want to get a drink?"

"Actually, I do. Alone."

"You don't really want to be alone."

"I don't want to be with you either."

"We're going to keep running into each other this weekend. Chances are good we'll play each other by late tomorrow. Let's enjoy tonight."

She finally stopped walking. "What do you want, Phin? Do you really think we're going to be friends?"

"What I really want to do is take you to bed."

"Sex isn't the answer to everything. It certainly won't fix the way you treated me."

"I'm sorry. I didn't want to hurt you, but I didn't know what else to do."

"You didn't need to do anything. If you didn't want me to stay with you, why didn't you just say so?" Her cheeks were red with anger, but her eyes softened with pain.

He ran a hand over the top of his head, suddenly missing his long hair. "I did want you to stay with me. I wanted you to stay more than you can ever understand."

"Funny way of showing it." She turned and walked onto the elevator.

He followed, searching for the right words. "You don't belong riding around aimlessly. You had a life waiting for you. I was spring-break fun."

She stared at her feet. "That's what it started out as, sure, but it became more. At least for me."

"For me too. You know that. You have to know that."

"I know nothing. For a week, you said as little as possible. When I told you I was looking for a job, you had your opening. All you had to say was, 'Go home, Layla.'"

The elevator dinged at her floor and he dogged her heels. "Would you have listened?"

"I guess we'll never know."

"Fuck that. We both know you would've gotten mad and taken off in some other direction. I knew telling you to leave wouldn't work. You were meant to finish college and have a great career. I couldn't offer you any of that. You're too smart to live my life."

She stood at the door to her room, key card poised. "I didn't ask you for anything."

"Bullshit. You were using me to run away from your life, but you wouldn't tell me why. I tried to talk to you and you got naked. You wouldn't tell me what you needed either."

"All I needed was you."

He set his cue case on the floor. "But you deserve more than that."

Phin touched her cheek and she leaned into his palm.

She pulled away. "I guess I should thank you. I finished school, and I'm really liking my life right now. This tournament . . . it's closure for me. Doing the best I can here will close the chapter on spring break."

She slipped the card into the lock and went in.

Phin wanted to believe he still had a chance, but every time they talked, Layla made it sound more and more final.

LAYLA CLOSED THE DOOR BEHIND HER AND SANK against it. She imagined a movie cutaway where Phin leaned on the opposite side. Pitiful. Walking away from Phin was getting harder and harder. She pushed off the door, showered and changed, and went in search of a cold beer.

For all of her brave words to Phin outside her room, she'd wanted to grab him and kiss him. Playing a game of pool at his side instead of against him had been a mistake, but she sure as shit hadn't wanted to play with either of the other two guys. She was surprised at how quickly she and Phin had fallen into that old rhythm of comfort. How could that be? They'd spent less than a week together two months ago.

Sitting at the hotel bar, she was draining the last of the beer in her third bottle when Phin arrived. Was there really no escape? "Are you stalking me now or what?"

"I suppose some might consider it stalking. I was looking for you, and if walking into every bar and restaurant attached to the hotel counts as stalking, then I'm guilty." He smiled, and she knew he wanted her to melt.

She nodded to the bartender to get another beer. "Confessions get you into trouble."

"I'm not worried."

Layla looked at him and tamped down the desire to wrap herself around him. "Maybe you should be."

He eased onto the stool beside her, his thigh brushing hers. "With you, I never worry."

The feeling was mutual, which just made her cranky again. She took a sip of her fresh beer and tried not to crumble under Phin's scrutiny. "What do you want, Phin?"

"I want to talk to you. Really talk. I thought I was never going to see you again and here you are. I don't want to miss this chance."

"There is no chance here and you suck at talking."

"I'm trying to get better. What do you want to know?"

So many thoughts and questions rattled through her head. She shook it clear. "Nothing. I wanted more of you two months ago and you offered nothing. I don't need anything from you now."

His finger traced a line on her thigh. "No, you never needed me, but the want is still pretty strong."

After slapping money on the bar, she twisted and hopped off the stool, leaving her beer behind.

"How about another game? For every ball you sink, I'll tell you something about myself."

Layla walked out of the bar without answering him. Of course he followed.

"What do you have to lose? We play a game; you might get my whole life story. Then if you still want me to back off, I will."

What did she have to lose? The last of her self-respect, the excellent buzz she had going on, a good night's sleep . . . her heart. She made the mistake of looking into his eyes. They were pleading in a way she couldn't comprehend. She couldn't really read his eyes, but they still conveyed feeling straight to her heart. His eyes always undid her, but with the lack of hair to fringe his face, they were even more powerful, if that was possible. There was nothing else to distract her and they sucked her in. "Why'd you cut your hair?"

"I needed a change. Figured it was time to grow up."

"Adults can't have long hair?"

He shrugged as if he wasn't so sure about the gesture now. "I needed a change."

"Why does it have to be a game? Why can't you just talk?"

Another shrug. "I wouldn't know where to start."

He looked so young and unsure of everything. His casual confidence nowhere to be found. She closed her eyes. He needed closure as much as she did. It couldn't hurt to hear him out. "Buy me a coffee and we'll talk. I'm buzzed and can't play pool."

His face lit up. "Wait here." He took off at a run to a kiosk that sold coffee. He returned with two large cups. "Where do you want to go?"

She blew into the brew. Knowing she'd probably regret it, she suggested his room. At least there, if things got too hairy, she could leave. They didn't say anything on the ride up to his floor, and Layla tried to form questions. What did she want to know about Phin that she didn't already?

It wasn't like she didn't care. She cared too much about him, but she felt like she knew him so well that the small details didn't matter. And weren't they all small details?

In his room, she steered clear of the bed and took the chair at the table. Phin paced the room carrying his coffee like a prop.

"Say your piece, Phin. I'm not going to spend the night here."

He huffed out a short breath. "When I left my family, I told myself it was because I wanted a normal life. I wanted what every other kid had: a house, a yard, a dad who worked a regular job, a girlfriend. I was angry that I didn't have that. But I had no idea what to do with myself. For the first two years on my own, I was basically homeless. I stole; I conned people; I slept in my truck. On my twentieth birthday I realized that I hadn't changed. I had given my father all this grief about the way I had been forced to live my life, but then I went out and did the same things. So I made a plan."

He sat on the edge of the bed. "I hit the tournament circuit to get money. All the other odd jobs I worked gave me spending money so I could eat. My tournament money is sitting in a bank. As soon as I had enough, I planned to pick a place and settle down. Find a regular job, mow the lawn, marry a nice girl."

"You said you didn't want to get married."

"Not at eighteen. My dad had my wife chosen for me at the age of twelve. He wanted to control everything because he was afraid I'd leave like my mom did."

Layla absorbed what Phin said, but found none of it surprising. She continued to watch him, let him say what he needed to say. None of it would change her mind. She wouldn't let it.

"Everything changed when I met you. I was still on that same treadmill as I'd been on for the first two years; it just paid better. I hadn't made any real plans. I was still jumping from town to town, hitting tournaments and playing pool for twenty bucks a pop. You had everything I ever wanted. You come from a normal family with parents who expected you to go to college, get a job, and move out. You have friends, real friends who you talk to all the time. But you took one look at my life and you were willing to walk away from all of it."

She set her coffee on the table. "It was my choice. It had nothing to do with you."

"Yeah, it did. You looked at me and saw adventure and fun. You didn't see the days of no shower for a week or picking someone's pocket in hopes of finding a couple of bucks for dinner." He rubbed a hand on his head. "I looked at you and saw my mom."

A laugh bubbled up. "That's kind of sick."

He squeezed his eyes shut. "Not like that. She met my father during a con and fell in love with him. She thought the lifestyle of a drifter was romantic. She never thought about how much she would miss having people outside the family to talk to. So she ran off. She left me out of desperation."

Phin crossed the space between them and squatted in front of her. "I never wanted you to be desperate to get away from me because I wouldn't be able to give you the kind of life you would want. I wasn't good enough for you and I knew it, so I drove you away."

"Well, that was a crappy way to handle everything. I'm old enough to make my own decisions, and if I screw up, that's on me. You don't owe me anything. We had a great week together." She inched forward in the chair with the intent to get up and leave. His story was over. He was sorry. So was she.

He rose to his feet. "Wait."

She stood and their bodies were practically

touching. Layla stared at his chest, remembering the feel of him under her hands.

Phin's hands cradled her jaw. "I want another chance to be the guy."

God, how she loved the way he touched her face, like she was delicate and beautiful. She licked her lips and asked, "What guy?"

"The guy who's good enough for you." Again, he lowered his lips to hers and kissed her gently, asking forgiveness and permission.

The walls around her heart crumbled and her chest hurt. It didn't make any sense. They didn't belong together. He'd been right about that, but when he held her and kissed her, it felt right.

He pulled away. "Can I ask you a question?"

She nodded.

"Why are you really here? You don't like pool that much."

Where to start? What could she tell him without becoming more vulnerable? She stepped away from him because she knew she'd be stronger without the weight of his arms for support. "I told you when we first met that I'm competitive. In Atlanta, you said I wasn't good enough. I needed to prove to myself that I am."

"What? Of all the crappy things I did that last day, that's the one that stands out for you? Why?" The look on his face was one of total bafflement.

There was no way he could possibly understand. She needed to know she could handle anything—his betrayal, the tournament, a new life. Besides, focusing her energy on becoming a better player kept the panic attacks at bay. She hadn't had one since leaving Atlanta. "Because I'm not the kind of person who fails. And for you to tell me that I wasn't good enough was like a failure. I'm here to redeem myself."

"So am I."

His words carried so much more weight than hers, but she couldn't explain why. "Good luck then."

"Stay with me." It came out as a cross between a plea and a command.

"I can't do that." She walked out the door to get a good night's sleep. She had to be on her game tomorrow. A day or two of playing pool and then back to the real world and her real life. One where there was no room for Phin.

PHIN DIDN'T SLEEP. AFTER HIS CONVERSATION WITH Layla, he realized how wrong he'd been. She'd tried using him to run from her life, but he'd been no better. He filled his life with excuses rather than sticking to his plan. His bank account held plenty to carry him into the next phase.

Last night, he'd decided that Layla was his next phase. They belonged together, and he was determined to make her see that. He was willing to walk away from everything to get her. In the early morning light, a plan developed.

He always played to win.

CHAPTER 10

*L*ayla's first game of the day was the following afternoon. Although a night of restlessness made her miss her practice time, she managed to win. Another round done. She might not be good enough to get into the finals and take home the purse—she was up against guys who'd been playing for years and did nothing but play pool—but she refused to go home after only two matches.

After her win, she scanned the area for Phin. She'd been sure he would show to watch her play. He'd shown up everywhere, but not when she made it into the semifinals. Phin's pals from the day before stood on the perimeter of the room, but he wasn't with them. She checked the schedule and saw that his game would be starting soon.

Grabbing a cup of coffee, she wandered the hall and watched a few matches, tried to pick out who she might face next. Then she saw Phin. He looked ragged. She stayed out of his line of sight, but watched.

When it was his turn, Phin barely looked at the table. He leaned over and took a careless shot. The three ball bounced around, clanking into other balls, going nowhere. What the hell was he doing? She'd never seen him take such a sloppy shot. Even his opponent looked shocked. It had been a rookie move. His opponent was good and Phin didn't care.

Then it hit her. He was throwing the game. He was giving up. She almost stormed over to the table to yell at him, but didn't want to get penalized for interference. She fumbled for her phone and sent him a text.

Stop fucking around and win.

He glanced at his phone and searched the crowd for her. She stepped forward and made eye contact. He shrugged.

I don't want to win because you quit. Then she added **Please.**

He checked the table and texted back. **Spend the night with me.**

They stared at each other from opposite sides of the table. He was going to coerce her into sleeping with him? She shouldn't care. She'd planned on playing at this tournament regardless of whether he showed. Why did she need to beat him?

Phin hopped off his chair and she realized it was his turn. He cocked an eyebrow, waiting for her answer as he approached the table.

She gave him a stiff nod.

Then he forgot about her presence as he attacked the table. The crowd around her closed in, amazed by the sudden turnaround. She didn't need to see; she knew he would win. Because Phin always played to win.

Had he known she was watching? Or had he really planned to give up? She backed away from the match and stood at the door. Moments later, Phin emerged from the crowd, people slapping his back as he cut through. He headed straight for her as if she wore a homing device.

As soon as he was close enough, her angry whisper tore through her. "What do you think you're doing?"

"Playing pool."

"No, you were giving up. Why?"

"My need to win doesn't matter. It's more important to you, so I'm willing to step aside." He shifted his case to his left hand.

"You can't let me win. That's the same as saying I'm not good enough to beat you."

He laughed quietly. "We both know you're not good enough to beat me."

"You're an asshole."

"We've already established that."

He stepped closer and she gripped her cue case with both hands, afraid to move.

"Let's go upstairs. They won't have results up until later this afternoon."

"I don't owe you my whole day, just the night." The thought of lying naked and sweaty with Phin made her warm all over.

"We'll be playing against each other sometime tonight. One of us has to lose. Are you still going to want to sleep with me after that?"

"Still? Who said I wanted to sleep with you now?"

He leaned close and sniffed her. "I can smell your desire. You want me every bit as much as I want you. You wanted closure. This is my closure."

"Fine." It would be the best good-bye sex she'd probably ever experience.

His eyes widened. He hadn't expected her to agree. She smiled and walked toward the elevator.

HOLY FUCK. HE'D NEVER THOUGHT SHE'D SAY YES. At best, he'd expected a "fuck you"; at worst, a slap across the face.

"Your room?" she asked.

They'd always been in his place. He wanted to know what Layla's place looked like, even though it was just a hotel room. "Let's go to yours."

Her eyebrows furrowed, but she pressed seven on the elevator.

She stood stiffly beside him, and he tried to come up with something to say.

"Why'd you agree?"

"To what?"

"Coming with me."

She snorted. "You haven't gotten me to come yet."

"But we both know I can. Again and again."

Color crept up her long neck. He wanted to

flick the buttons open on her blouse. He'd never pictured her in anything but jeans and T-shirts, and this version of Layla was a turn-on. All professional and shit. He imagined her in an office and then thought of fucking her on the desk. He shifted and adjusted himself as the elevator arrived on seven.

Inside her room she placed her case on the dresser and he laid his beside it. Then she stripped. No pretense, no games. In less than a minute she was wearing nothing more than a bra and panties.

"In a hurry?"

"You wanted good-bye sex. What's the point in messing around? Let's get to the sex so we can get to the good-bye."

She had no idea what she was in for. He'd thought about it for the last two months. Over the last two days, he'd pictured this moment. He might not have a way with words, but he'd show her how he felt. What she meant to him.

Everything. He wanted to give and take it all. He just hoped that he held on to enough patience to go as slow as he knew he needed to.

Layla closed the distance and wrapped her arms around his neck. Her kiss was harsh and lusty. She was a girl looking to get laid. He grabbed the back of her neck and slowed the pace of the kiss, but she rammed her hips against his thigh.

"This is my idea, my time, my way," he whispered against her lips.

"And now you have a problem with the way I

kiss you?"

"Only because you're in a rush and I plan on taking my time with you to savor every last taste . . . moan . . . quiver." His hands grazed over her bare stomach and the muscles twitched, giving him plenty of satisfaction. He held her hand and pulled her toward the bed. He sat on the edge and kissed his way down her torso and across her hipbone.

Her hands held his shoulders. For purchase or to have the ability to shove him away, he wasn't sure, but when he sucked on her nipple through her bra, her nails dug into his skin, and her thighs tensed. She tried to shove him back onto the bed, but he turned and had her beneath him instead.

He continued to kiss her face, her neck, her breasts, her stomach, until she was panting and wiggling against his thigh. She tried to grab his crotch, but he moved out of her reach.

"Come on, Phin. Get naked. It's more fun when both of us are naked and sweaty."

"We'll get there." He unclasped her bra and slid it off. He traced the line of her panties across her stomach, and she raised her hips to give him a hint. He tugged the damp panties off and touched her. Her hips bucked at the first stroke, but he wanted more. She smelled so good, so tempting. He lowered his head and kissed her thigh, working his way up.

She suddenly jolted up. "What are you doing?"

"I said I wanted to go down on you."

"But you don't do that." Her eyes were wide

and panicked.

"Don't you like it?"

"Uh . . ."

"Lie back and relax." He shoved her shoulder gently and pulled her hips to his face. He'd watched enough porn to have an idea of what to do. He ran his tongue along the length of her slit and tasted the tang of her arousal. His dick throbbed in response. His lips brushed against her and she moaned. "Let me know if I do something you don't like."

"Uh-huh."

He chuckled against her, causing another moan. He licked and sucked and thrust his tongue into her. When he tugged her clit and sucked hard, her body stiffened. He released and looked up across her naked body. "Not good?"

"Too." She released a gasp. "Good. Don't. Stop."

So he didn't. Her hands gripped his scalp, pulling at the short hair, and she threw her legs over his shoulders, guiding him into her. His tongue and fingers worked her and moved away and brought her to the brink until she was whimpering.

And then she broke, screaming his name along with God's, and her muscles clenched and trembled. When she released him, he crawled over her, his dick so hard it hurt, so he couldn't get naked. Not yet.

He smoothed her hair away from her face and allowed his fingers to touch her face until she opened her eyes. He smirked. "I think I did pretty good for my first time, but I might need some more practice.”

The panic hadn't left her face, but she tried to cover it. “Fuck you, Phin. Glad I could be your guinea pig. You nailed it. Hurray for you.” Then she added a saucy grin. “Yay for me too, because that was one helluva orgasm.”

“Ready for another?”

“Always.” She said it like a dare.

He stripped and put on a condom. He covered her body with his, and she closed her eyes as she wrapped her legs around his hips. His cock was poised at her entrance and he wanted to bury himself.

“Look at me, Layla.”

Her throat worked and her eyes fluttered open.

He inched into her slowly, and, with every slight movement, he broke away another piece of the barrier she'd constructed around her heart. Once he was all the way in, he stopped and relished the feel of her surrounding him completely. He lowered his head and kissed her neck. With his face tucked into that soft spot, he slid out and back in, creating a smooth rhythm.

“Why were you willing to walk away from your life to be with me?” he whispered in her ear. He wanted to know, needed to know that she loved him.

“It had nothing to do with you.”

He paused midstroke and raised up on his elbows to see her eyes. “Really?”

“Well, spending time with you was fun, but

you weren't the deciding factor."

"What was?"

The wall in her eyes shuttered. "Are we going to fuck or have a conversation?"

"Both." He slid all the way in and stopped again, pressing against her clit with his pelvic bone. She tried to squirm, looking for the second orgasm he'd promised her. "Tell me, Layla, and I'll let you come." He ground against her again and she groaned.

He stared into her eyes, needing her to see his sincerity, needing to see the real Layla without her armor and sarcasm. "Please. I want to know."

"I had a panic attack and I didn't want to go back. That was it."

Those were not words he'd expected. He didn't know what he had expected, but it wasn't that. Layla was so together; he couldn't imagine her having a panic attack.

"Fuck me now, or get the hell off." Her words bit at him.

He began thrusting again and allowed her to meet him. When she was close, he backed off and reached between them and pressed his thumb against her clit. He watched her shatter for a second time and then followed her.

They lay on the bed, chests heaving, muscles lax. Phin didn't want to move. He wanted to continue holding her, but she smacked his arm. "Off," she grunted.

As soon as he rolled to the side, she scooted out from under him and went to the bathroom without so much as a glance in his direction.

"I'm going to take a shower. I'll see you downstairs."

Wait. She was throwing him out? "Tell me about the panic attack."

"No deal. You said you'd continue to really play if I slept with you. You got what you wanted, plus a bonus answer to a question simply because I really wanted to come again. I'm not giving you any more."

She closed the door behind her, and he sat up when he heard the water running. He wouldn't walk away. He'd chosen her room so that she couldn't either. They would figure this out now or neither of them would make it to the tournament.

LAYLA STOOD UNDER THE HOT SPRAY OF THE WATER feeling raw and exposed. She didn't regret the sex because she'd known that would be great, but it was supposed to be good-bye sex and he'd made it feel like make-up sex. Or welcome home sex. She couldn't believe that he'd gotten her so wound up that she'd told him about her panic attacks. She'd never told anyone about them except for her therapist and Charlie and Felicity. People who wouldn't judge her.

After she'd told Phin, she'd seen the look in his eyes. Knew he'd never look at her the same. She was broken, and he couldn't reconcile that image with the girl he knew. She understood that because she couldn't reconcile that part of her with who she knew herself to be. Panic attacks made her feel weak, like less of a person because she couldn't control them.

When the bathroom was filled with steam and she was sure Phin would've given up on waiting for her, she stepped from the shower and wrapped a towel around herself. She opened the door and the steam billowed out, leading the way into the now-dark room.

Shit. Phin was still there. He'd pulled his pants back on, but sat against the headboard of her bed.

He looked at her with a smirk. "I don't give up that easily."

She hated that he saw through her. "Get out of my room."

"Not until you talk to me. You're quick to point out my shortcomings in the communication department, and yet you failed to mention that you have panic attacks."

"A panic attack." She didn't really count the one on the way down to Georgia. It hadn't become a full attack.

"I've never heard of a random, out-of-the-blue panic attack."

"Don't care."

"Talk to me, Layla."

"No." She went to the dresser and pulled out fresh panties and a bra. She dropped the towel and dressed in front of Phin. When she slid her arm into her blouse, he came up behind her and held out the other sleeve, and then proceeded to button her up. All she could do was stare.

"I want to know you like you want to know

me. Aside from having amazing sex with you, I like who I am with you, and I think you feel the same. Why are you fighting it?"

"Because . . ." Tightness in her chest began building. Why was she fighting it? Wasn't this what she'd wanted from Phin two months ago? If he had opened up then . . . She would've left school and disappointed her parents. Would've abandoned an awesome job offer. "You were right in Atlanta. As much as I loathe admitting it, I was crazy to think that following you all over the country was a good idea. I have my life and you have yours. We had a great spring break."

His thumb stroked her cheek. "We can have more."

"How? You'll never look at me as your equal, and I won't settle for anything less. Am I supposed to sit around waiting for you to blow through town to give me a night of your time before you leave again?" She inhaled slowly, filling her lungs to capacity, refusing to let panic take hold. But then she realized it wasn't panic, but plain old fear.

She didn't know if she was more afraid that Phin would walk away, or that he wouldn't.

"Layla." His voice coasted over her, wrapping her in comfort. "I wanted this last tournament for the money. That's all. This last purse isn't going to make or break me; it was just the threshold I named for my plans and myself. The last one, the last big win."

"Why?"

"Because I picked a random number that represented what I would need to buy a house and fill it with furniture and appliances."

She shook her head. "No. Why were you willing to throw the last game and walk away from your goal?"

He ran his hands up and down her arms. "If I don't win, I give up what? Maybe getting a huge TV? A leather couch? None of that matters. You do. I don't want to take anything from you. You've worked hard to be able to get into this tournament."

"But by not playing, you are taking that away from me. I can live with losing to you." Again. Maybe.

"I don't want you to lose to me. I don't want to play against you. I like it better when we're on the same side."

He pulled her to him and held her. She heard his heart beating a steady rhythm under his smooth skin. She loved the feel of him, the smell of him, and relaxed in his arms.

"I think I love you," he whispered.

Her breath froze in her lungs. She hadn't expected that. She started to pull away, but he held her tight.

"Shh . . . I don't know if it's love because I've never been here before. But I do know that when you left, I couldn't think straight. I wanted to call you and apologize, but I knew it wouldn't be fair. I tried to accept that I had fucked up and lost you."

He stroked her back and all logical thought fled from her brain.

"You're amazing and we're not equals. You're

better than I am, and I've always known that. I don't know how you didn't see it."

They were both messed up, and she felt better realizing it. Against his chest, she mumbled, "You're wrong."

He released her so he could look at her face. She saw he was ready for an argument.

Layla wrapped her arms around his neck and kissed him. "You're him. You're the guy. Deep down I felt it, but didn't pay attention. I've never been more myself than I am with you."

"Does that mean I won?"

"Won what?"

"You."

"You never really lost me." She curled back into his arms. "What do we do now?"

"First, we go win the tournament."

"And then?"

"Then I follow you wherever you want to go," Phin said.

"Really?"

"I want to plant my roots near you."

This time, when her chest tightened, Layla was happy. Her heart swelled and raced and part of her felt like it might burst, but it was an excellent feeling. Phin picked her up and carried her back to bed.

Suddenly making it back to the tournament was unimportant. She'd already won.

Keep reading for a special excerpt from chapter one of *Her Perfect Game,* Charlie's story. And don't miss Felicity's spring break adventure in *Her Winning Formula*!

If you could spare a moment, I would appreciate you leaving a review of this book.

If you'd like to stay up-to-date on my releases and have the chance to win some prizes, click here to join my newsletter.

If you liked *Her Best Shot,* be sure to check out my contemporary romance series, The O'Learys:

More Than This
A Good Time
Something to Prove
Catch Your Breath
Just a Taste
Hold Me Close

Charlie walked through her apartment, keenly aware of the quiet. Her roommate Amy usually left the TV or the radio playing. Sometimes both. Charlie glanced to the kitchen counter and saw two wine glasses sitting near the sink.

Oh goody, Amy had her boyfriend over. Again. Charlie was trying not to be a bitch about it, but the man was in their place more than Charlie was, and he wasn't paying for anything. What made it worse was that he'd eat her food, like her favorite yogurt, and then not even have the decency to offer a fake apology.

She yanked her hair free from her ponytail and kicked her shoes off, nudging them close to the door so she could easily find them in the morning. Work had beaten her down tonight. As much as she hated the morning shift at a coffee shop, she could at least understand why people might be rude to her. She tended to land on the far side of testy without her morning dose of caffeine. But at seven in the evening?

Tonight had been one of those nights when she could do nothing right. Even if she thought it had been right, the customers didn't agree. All she wanted was a hot shower and some time to play *The Order of Resskaar*. As she grabbed her pajamas from her room, she heard quiet moans coming from the other side of the wall she shared with Amy.

Good thing Charlie owned an excellent pair of headphones. Her dry spell would make hearing Amy and her boyfriend go at it difficult at best. Charlie didn't like being jealous, but it had been way too long since she'd experienced a screaming orgasm, regardless of what her good friends believed.

Part of that was because Ethan had never hit the mark that some men did. He hadn't been a bad lover, exactly, just not as good as others. She sighed and started the hot water. She needed to flush men from her mind. Only two months remained in the school year, and then she wouldn't be able to hold her secret anymore.

Telling everyone—her mom, Layla, Felicity— that she had dropped out of school would sting a whole lot less if she at least had a plan figured out. Having time to implement that plan would be even better.

After her shower, Charlie went back to her room and tuned out the sounds of the squeaky bed banging against the wall. She booted up her computer and put on her headphones. She hoped Win was online because she could really use a friend tonight. He'd take her mind off her lame job and whiny customers. And if it was a quiet night, maybe they could sneak away for some private time.

So much for flushing men from her mind.

But Win didn't count. He was a virtual man. Well, she was pretty sure he was a man in the real world too, but she only knew him virtually, as a dwarven mage. And it would stay that way unless she could finally convince him to join her at the convention. They would have so much fun together. Even outside the bedroom.

As the home screen welcomed her, Charlie began to relax. She turned the volume up on her stereo to drown out Amy's noise. She preferred to listen to music while she played and just read the conversation on screen. In her head, the characters had natural voices, and the computerized versions never sounded real enough, so she ignored them.

She shot a message to Win. *You around?*

No one answered, so she wandered through the virtual forest looking for the rest of the members of her guild. At least two others were logged on. As she walked, she noticed that her friends had picked up some treasures while she'd been at work. Looking at the loot, she saw things that they had all agreed were unnecessary for their mission. She sighed. This happened every now and then, especially when new members joined the guild.

She didn't try to restrict membership, but she

had guidelines for what she expected the group to be. They were called The Guardians after all. Stealing from people and taking things they didn't need went against everything they stood for. She searched for the tree that would have the items tied to the boughs out of sight. When she found the bag, she took it with her to the village. Starting at the orphanage, she handed out items that others would use to barter to stay alive.

That's when she ran into Kraven. He was the newest member of the guild, and she suspected he was the one responsible for the bag.

What are you doing? That's my stuff.

I'm spreading the wealth. That's what we do.

Do you know how many people I had to go up against to earn that?

I have no idea. What were you planning to do with it?

Save it to exchange for things we'll need. There are only a few more missions until we reach the final one. We'll need supplies to help Resskaar.

I'm in no hurry to reach the final battle. I told you that when you asked to join my guild.

Your guild? I assumed it was Win's guild. He was the one who invited me.

Win invited you after talking to me.

Figures. I'm out. Kraven snatched the bag from her hand and took off with whatever of his loot remained. He sneered at a few of the villagers, but he knew better than to take what she had just given them.

Confronting Kraven left a bad taste in her mouth. She'd come to the game tonight to find refuge, not a fight. Now, however, a fight might make her feel better. She checked the mission status. The others from her guild had logged off, except Kraven. She was on her own. She marched to the edge of town and took off in a run to find the band of marauders she knew had taken up camp.

The thieves stormed every village they came across until they left nothing but a shell behind. She knew she wouldn't be able to take them all on, but her health was near one hundred percent, so she could handle a couple before retreating.

In the distance, she saw the small campfire. As she neared the edge of the camp, she crept along the tree line. If she could find the right vantage point, she could take out half the group without breaking a sweat. Spotting a low-hanging branch, she jumped and climbed. When she found a good bough, one with enough coverage to hide her but still allow a clean shot with her arrow, she settled in. As she surveyed the group below her, a ping told her one of her guild had just logged on.

Win.

It was silly that her heartbeat quickened at the sight of his name, but every time she saw it, it was like she knew she'd be able to see a good friend.

Hey, gorgeous, where are you? Not in our cave.

She typed back quickly. *In a tree about to cause some trouble. Want to join me?*

On my way.

That was one of the many reasons she loved Win. He didn't ask questions; he just came. She got comfortable on her branch while she waited for him and developed a plan. She knew which men she'd need to take out first, and now that Win would have her back, she could attack and he could swoop in and take their cache.

By the end of her night, she'd at least make a few other people secure, and that might be enough to make up for her evening.

Moments later, she saw the rustle of a bush and knew Win had arrived. He always knew where to find her. She launched her first arrow, nailing one soldier's shoulder. She'd taken out two more before the others realized what was happening. Unfortunately, they figured out quickly where she was and came at her.

She jumped from her branch and led them away from Win's position. Without the rest of their guild, he didn't stand a chance against these monsters. She might be able to outrun them. It seemed like a good plan until one shot a rock and hit her in the head. A breath later they were on her, kicking her and throwing more stones. Her life energy was waning fast. She tried to scramble to her feet, but it was no use. They outnumbered her and had her surrounded.

Suddenly a flash fire burst around her and she sighed. If it had been the enemy, she'd be in flames. This was Win's doing. The group tossed a few more rocks in her direction, but gave up when they realized that it wasn't worth the health points to get past the fire.

Thanks for having my back.

That was a stupid move. You okay?

Been better.

Then the flames died and Win stood there staring at her, a stuffed bag flung over his shoulder. The mission was a success.

Come on. He leaned over to pick her up.

In the quiet of her bedroom, Charlie laughed out loud. Win was a dwarf, a short, round guy about half her height. He was strong, though, and he hefted her and ran back to their cave.

You need to be more careful, Laura.

Win almost never called her by name. It suddenly struck her as weird. She called him Win all the time, but he never called her Laura.

They didn't speak again until they were safe and Win healed her. He was always doing that, taking care of her. Not that she didn't do her share of saving his ass, but he was a healer and she was a warrior. They made a hell of a team.

When she had regained her strength, she sat in front of the fire Win had built for them.

Have you thought about coming to the con next week?

I told you, I don't know if I can.

If it's money, you can crash in my room. All you need is registration.

We'll see.

She winked at him. *It'll be fun.* Then she curled up to sleep. Win lay beside her and everything in her calmed.

If only she had that in real life.

Meeting His Match

<u>Daring Divorcees Series</u>

One Night with a Millionaire

My Best Friend's Ex

My Forever Plus-One